It is a well known fact that only a healthy body keeps the healthy mind and pure heart. A person with good physical health can perform any physical, mental or spritual task without any difficulty. Physical unfitness leads to failure on all other fronts.

Regular and systematic physical exercise results into great contributions to body fitness and good health.

Sports and games are the best form of physical exercise. They are well regulated & well defined, hence they are uniform and systematic. Games and sports have too many advantages. Beside entertainment, they make us desciplined, organized, co-operating, and pertinent. They make up competetive and capable to work in a team, not only in field, but everywhere.

This book puts forward the historical aspects of certain games & sports and further educate about rules and regulation of respective games. Certainly, this book will promote your awareness about the different sports events, and enhance your interest as well.

Rules of Various Sports

Sanjay Bhola 'Dheer'

DIAMOND BOOKS

ISBN : 81-288-1544-X

© Publisher

Published by	:	**Diamond Pocket Books (P) Ltd.**
		X-30, Okhla Industrial Area, Phase-II
		New Delhi-110020
Phone	:	011-41611861-65, 40712100
Fax	:	011-41611866
E-mail	:	sales@dpb.in
Website	:	www.dpb.in
Edition	:	2009
Printed by	:	Star Print-O-Bind, Okhla, New Delhi-20

RULES OF VARIOUS SPORTS
By: *Sanjay Bhola 'Dheer'*

Dedicated to

Dear father,
loving mother
and
Kushal

Preface

Once, some young men went to Swami Vivekanand and asked, "Swami Ji! Tell us the actual meaning of the holy *Geeta.*" Swami Vivekanand replied, "My dear young men! It's not the time to know about the holy *Geeta.* Go to that ground and play football. By this you can not only build up your body, this will also help to make your legs and muscles strong and then you can easily understand about the spirit of holy *Geeta.*"

Today, the various types of sports usually come under physical exercises. By this we can not only keep our body fit but also can live a disciplined life. There may be lot of persons who wanted to became a physical educator or a famous sports personality like Sachin Tendulkar, Dhanraj Pillay, Sania Mirza, Milka Singh, P.T. Usha, Major Dhyanchand, Karnam Malleshwari, Vijay Amritraj, Vishwanathan Anand etc.

The book in your hand will help you as a 'treasure house' of sports. Children who acquire good knowledge in their tender years can be an asset to their nation.

We have introduced sports and games in as detailed a manner as possible. We hope also to create a uniquely valuable reference work that might serve individuals, families, schools, colleges and clubs. The study with the constantly changing nature of our knowledge on sports should make this a most interesting volume both for now and for years to come.

Grateful acknowledgements to Mr Narender Kumar Verma, Chairman, Diamond Pocket Books, for his guidance in editing this book and to 'Mamta' for assistance in preparing the manuscript.

—**Sanjay Bhola 'Dheer'**

Contents

Cricket

History

The name of the game, cricket, has always been synonymous with the notion of fair play and this reputation still persists, alongside its growing high-profile, commercial appeal. Cricket is the game of kings and the king of games. For many enthusiasts cricket is a way of life. Like all bat-and-ball games, cricket evolved gradually from various sources. It is related to an early Scottish sport known as '*Cat and Dog*', although the game itself, in some form, is thought to date back to the 13th century.

There was a time when cricket playing was banned by the Royal Order in England in twelth or thirteenth century. But the game's peculiar charm—its unpredictability — could not be denied its rightful place in the hearts of the Englishmen. So, wherever the Englishmen went, they spread the game and its popularity. The Hambeldon Club was founded in 1750. It was superseded by the Marylebone Cricket Club with its headquarters at Lords (London). This became the world authority of cricket and its sanctuary. In 1909, the Imperial Cricket Conference (I.C.C.) was framed and cricket became an international game. In 1956 the name of Imperial Cricket Conference was changed into International Cricket Conference.

In India, cricket was introduced by the British around 18th century. Indians took keen interest in the game particularly in the cities of Bombay, Calcutta, and Madras. The presidency matches began in 1892-93 between Parsis and Europeans and the tournament became the Bombay Triangular. India started the Ranji Trophy in 1935 by the efforts of several princes, H.E. Grant-Goven and A.S. de Mellow and till date the game is gaining higher values in the hearts of its fans.

Cricket Creases

The bowling crease is marked in line with the stumps, 8-ft 8 inch in length, with the stumps at the centre. The popping crease is parallel to this. It is marked 4 ft from the centre of the stumps and extends at least 6 ft on either side of the line of the wicket. The return crease is at right angles to the bowling crease. It is marked at least 4 ft behind the wicket and must be considered to be of unlimited length.

Cricket Pitch

The area between the two side wickets is called pitch. The width of pitch must be 10 ft, with the centre line being that which joins the two middle stumps. (For a non-turf pitch the dimensions are minimum length 58 ft and minimum width 6 ft with the same distance between the stumps, i.e. 22 yards.) The pitch shall not be changed during a match unless it becomes unfit for play and that too with the consent of both captains. It shall not be watered during a match.

Equipments

Wicket: Two sets of wickets (three stumps in each set) shall be pitched opposite and parallel to each other at a distance of 20.12 m (22 yards) between the centre of the two middle stumps. Each wicket shall be 22.80 cm in width. The stumps shall be of equal size and so as to prevent the ball from passing through, with their top 28 inches above the field. Two wooden bails shall be kept on the top of the stumps. Each bail must be 4-3/8 inch long and shall not project more than 1.3 cm above the stumps.

Bat: A cricket bat is made up of willow wood. It must be flat from one side for hitting the ball and the other side rounded. The blade of the bat is covered with a laminated material. The handle is made with cane and is covered with rubble or such material. The maximum length of bat must be not more than 38 inch (96.5 cm) and the blade must not exceed 4¼ inch (10.8 cm) at its widest part. A bat has a normal weight of 2 1b 10 oz.

Ball: A cricket ball is spherical which is cased in stitched red leather. It is made of cork and has the weight of 5½ -5¾ oz (155.9-163 gm). The circumference of the ball must be between 18-13/16 -19 inch (22.4-22.9 cm). In the event of the ball being lost or becoming unfit for play, the umpires shall allow another ball of the similar wear or use. The batsman should be informed whenever the ball is to be changed.

Sight-Screens: Sight-screens are a special kind of screen which are used to give batsman a clear view of the bowler and are positioned behind each wicket and outside the playing area, but close to the boundary line.

Gloves: Two types of gloves are used in the cricket match: One, which is used by a batsman during the striking. A batsman is allowed to wear the gloves made of smooth cotton or rexine with a thick cotton foam padding on the finger's outer side. This is to avoid injury to the fingers and wrist. Another kind of glove is wicketkeeping gloves. These gloves are used by a wicketkeeper during the fielding of a team. The inner gloves are made of cotton and wicketkeeping gloves (gauntlets) are made of soft leather. The wicketkeeping gloves protect the wicketkeeper from injury while catching, or stopping the ball.

Leg guards: Leg guards protect the batsmen and wicket-keeper from injury to leg while striking or stopping the ball. The leg guards are made of cotton with foam /cotton pad on the outer surface of them. The wicketkeeping guards are a little smaller than the batting guards.

Abdomen Protector: This safety equipment is worn by the batsmen and the wicket keepers to avoid any injury to genitals and abdomen. The protector is made up of solid plastic or such materials. It is very much light in weight. The protector is worn with the help of a plastic strip.

Helmet & Face guard: The only non-traditional items in the professional cricketer's dress are helmet and face guard. These are often worn as protection from fast or dangerous balls. The helmets are made with hard plastic or steel with a foam padding.

Dresses: All the players are required to wear white trousers, shirt, shoes and sweaters (with team colours as a trim) for test matches. Wearing of colour outfit is essential for one-day matches. The wicketkeeper must wear leg pad and protective gloves and the batsman must wear leg pads, gloves and protective helmet with a face guard.

Umpires: Two umpires are appointed to control the game. One umpire is located at the bowling wicket and the second one is standing square on to batting wicket. The positions of both the umpires are change after completion of each over. Before starting the match, both umpires shall satisfactorily check the field and wickets whether they are properly pitched or not. The umpies shall declare that the batsman is out or not, ensure bowling is within the rules and the game is fair or not. All the disputes shall be determined by the umpires. There is also a third umpire who does not act in the field but gives some important decisions. When both the umpires are not fully satisfied for taking any decision, they take from the third umpire. The decision is given by the camera, recording the match. It replays the situation occurred before any decision and gives the result by the green light as not out and red light as out.

Duration: A test match is consisting of one or two innings per team according to the agreement reached before the start of the play. An inning is completed when all the players of a team have been out or the batting captain 'declares' or is satisfied with the number of overs that have been bowled. Test matches runs for five days, with a maximum of 30 hours play. The duration of one-day match varies according to the standard of the match. There may be a limited playing time and the number of overs to be bowled. Normally one-day match requires to bowl 50 overs by each team and the batting team is free to score as maximum runs as it can. The team scoring the higher score than the other team is the winner. One-day matches are played at both international and first class level.

Starting: The captains of both the teams toss for the choice of the innings (i.e. to bat or to bowl first). When the umpire has called 'play', the fielding team position themselves across the ground while the two opening batsmen from the opposite team take their place in front of each wicket. A player of the fielding team bowls from the one end of the pitch to the batsman and thus the game starts on.

Scoring: The score shall be reckoned by runs. A run is scored: (i) So often as the batsman after a hit, or at any time while the ball is in play, shall have crossed and made good their ground from end to end, but if either batsman runs a short run, the umpire shall call a signal 'short one' and that run shall not be scored. The striker being caught, no run shall be scored, a batsman being run out, no run shall be scored.

(ii) An umpire signals short run when the ball becomes 'dead' by bending his arm upward to touch the shoulder with the tips of his fingers. If there has been more than one short the umpire must instruct the scorers as to the numbers of runs disallowed.

Boundaries and Sixers

An umpire shall call or signal 'boundary' whenever, in his opinion, a ball in the play hits, crosses or is carried over the boundary line. The runs completed at the instant the ball reaches the boundary shall not count should they exceed the allowance, but if the boundary results from an overthrow or from the wilful act of a fielder, any runs already made and the allowance shall be added to the score. The customary allowance for a bounbdary is 4 runs, but it is usual to allow 6 runs for all hits pitching over and clearing the boundary line or fence even though the ball has been previously touched by a fielder. The umpire signals 'boundary' by waving an arm from side to side or a boundary '6' by raising both arms above the head.

No-Ball

When the umpire is not entirely satisfied with the bowling of any delivery by the bowler, he may call the signal of 'no-ball'. During the delivery, if the bowler's front foot ends up beyond the popping crease or the bowler's back foot is outside the return crease, both are bowling faults and no-balls. The batsman may hit a no-ball and make runs from it, but he can only be dismissed by being run out. If a batsman is unable to make any runs from a no-ball, one run is added to his team.

Wide Ball

If the bowler bowls the ball so high or so wide of the wicket that in the opinion of the umpire it passes out of reach of the batsman, standing in a normal guard position, then the umpire shall call and signal 'wide ball' as soon as it has passed through the line of the batsman's wicket. A penalty of one run for a wide ball shall be scored if no runs are made otherwise. A batsman may be out if he handles the ball, obstruct the field or hits wickets, stumped and run out.

Bye and Leg Bye

If the ball, not having been called "wide" or "no-ball", passes the batsman without touching his bat or him, and any runs are obtained, the umpire shall signal 'bye' and the run or runs shall be credited as much to the batting team. If the ball, not having been called a 'wide' or 'no-ball' is unintentionally deflected by the batsman's dress or him, except the hand holding the bat and any runs are obtained, the umpire shall signal 'leg bye' and the run or runs scored shall be credited as such to a batting team. Such leg bye shall be scored if, in the opinion of the umpire, the batsman has:

(i) attempted to play the ball with his bat

(ii) tried to avoid being hit by the ball.

Appeals

The umpires shall not give a batsman out unless appealed to by the other side, which shall be done prior to the bowler beginning his run-up or bowling action to deliver the next ball. The ball is dead on 'over' being called; this does not, however, invalidate an appeal made prior to the first ball of the following over provided 'time' has not been called. An appeal 'How's that?' shall cover all ways of being out.

Wicket Is Down

The wicket is down if:

(i) Either the ball or the batsman's bat or person completely removes either bails from the top of the stumps. A disturbance of a bail whether temporary or not, shall not constitute a complete removal, but the wicket is down if a bail in falling lodges between two of the stumps.

(ii) Any player completely removes with his hand or arm a bail from the top of the stumps, provided that the ball is held in that hand or in hand of the arm so used.

(iii) When both the bails are off, a stump is struck out of the ground by the ball or a player strikes or pulls a stump out of the ground, provided that the ball is held in the hand or in the hand of the arm so used.

Batsman Out Of His Ground

A batsman shall be considered to be out of his ground unless some part of his bat in his hand or of his person is grounded behind the line of the popping crease.

Bowled

A batsman shall be out bowled if:

(i) His wicket is bowled down, even if the ball first touches his bat or a person.

(ii) He breaks his wicket by hitting or kicking the ball on to it before the completion of a stroke, or as a result of attempting to guard his wicket.

(iii) A batsman is not bowled if the ball is deflected on to his wicket even though a decision against him would be justified by the law.

Timed Out

A batsman is timed out while incoming the field if he wilfully takes more than two minutes to come in. The two minutes being from the moment a wicket falls until the new batsman steps on the field of the play. If this is not complied with and if the umpire is satisfied that the delay was wilful and if an appeal is made, the new batsman shall be given out by the umpire at the bowler's end.

Caught

A batsman shall be caught if the ball touches his bat or if it touches below the wrist of his hand or glove holding the bat, and is subsequently held by any fielder before it touches the ground. A catch shall be considered to have been fairly made if:

(i)   The fielder is within the field of play throughout the act of making the catch.

(ii)   The act of making the catch starts from the time when the fielder first handles the ball and shall end when he both retains complete control over the further disposal of the ball and remains within the field of play.

(iii) In order to be within the field of play, the fielder may not touch or ground any part of his person on or over a boundary line. When the boundary is marked by a fence or board the fielder may not ground any part of his person over the boundary fence or board, but may touch or lean over the boundary fence or board in completing the catch.

Handled the Ball

Either batsman on appeal shall be out 'handled the ball' if he wilfully touches the ball while in play with his hand not holding the bat unless he does so with the consent of the opposite side. The hand holding the bat is regarded as part of it for the purpose of laws. The correct entry in the score book when a batsman is given out under this law is "handled the ball" and the bowler does not get credit for the wicket.

Hit the Ball Twice

A batsman is out "hit the ball twice" if the ball be struck or be stopped by any part of his person and he wilfully strikes it again, except for the sole purpose of guarding his wicket, which he may do with his bat or any part of his body other than his hand. No runs except those which result from an overthrow shall be scored from a ball lawfully struck twice.

The striker, on appeal, shall be out under this law, if without the consent of the opposite side, he uses his bat or person to return the ball to any of the fielding side. No runs except those which result from an overthrow or penalty shall be scored from a ball lawfully struck twice.

Hit Wicket

A batsman shall be out 'hit wicket', if, while the ball is in play:

(i) His wicket is broken with any part of his person, dress or equipment as a result of any action taken by him in preparing to receive or in receiving a delivery or in setting off for his first run, immediately after playing or playing at the ball.

(ii) He hits down his wicket whilst lawfully making a second stroke for the purpose of guarding his wicket within the provisions of law.

A batsman is not out for breaking the wicket with his bat or body while in the act of running.

LBW (Leg Before Wicket)

A batsman shall be out L.B.W. in the circumstances given below:

(i) If the batsman first intercepts with any part of his person, dress or equipment a fair ball which would have hit the wicket and which has not previously touched his bat or a hand holding the bat.

(ii) If the ball is intercepted outside the line of the off-stump, if, in the opinion of the umpire, he has made a genuine attempt to play the ball with his bat, but has intercepted the ball with some part of his person and if the other circumstances set out in.

Obstructing the Field

A batsman, on appeal, shall be out 'obstructing the field' if he wilfully obstructs the opposite side by word or action.

The batsman, on appeal, shall be out should wilful obstruction by either batsman prevents a catch being made. This shall apply even though the striker causes the obstruction in lawfully guarding his wicket under the provisions of law.

Run Out

Either batsman is out 'run out' if in running or at any time, while the ball is in play, he may be out of the ground and his wicket may be put down by any fielder or wicket-keeper. If the batsmen have crossed each other, and one of them then runs for the wicket which is put down is out. If they have not crossed, then he that has left the wicket which is put down is out. But unless he attempts to run, the batsman shall not be given 'run-out' in the circumstances stated in the law, even if 'no-ball' has been called.

If the ball is played on to the opposite wicket, neither batsman is liable to be 'run-out' unless the ball has been touched by a fielder before the wicket is put down.

Stumped

A batsman shall be 'stumped' out if, in receiving the ball, not being a no-ball, he is out of his ground otherwise than in attempting a run and his wicket is put down by the wicket-keeper without the intervention of another fielder.

The wicket-keeper may take the ball in front of the wicket in an attempt to stump the batsman only if the ball has touched the bat or the person of the batsman.

The Fielders

A fielder may stop the ball with any part of his person, but if he wilfully stops it otherwise, five runs shall be added to the run or runs already scored; if no runs have been scored five penalty runs shall be awarded to the batting team. If the ball has been struck, the penalty shall be added to the score of the batsman, but otherwise to the score of byes, leg-byes, no-balls or wides as the case may be. A fielder can not use his cap for the purpose of fielding a ball. If any fielder is using protective helmet, when it is not in use, it shall only be placed, if above the surface, on the ground behind the wicket-keeper. If the ball is striking the helmet, five penalty runs shall be awarded.

The Wicket-keeper

The wicket-keeper shall remain wholly behind the wicket until a ball delivered by the bowler touches the bat or person of the batsman or passes the wicket, or until the batsman attempts a run. The umpire at the striker's end shall call and signal 'no-ball' in the event of wicket-keeper contravening this law. If the wicket-keeper interferes with the batsman's right to play the ball and to guard his wicket, the batsman shall not be out, except under laws. If in the legitimate defence of his wicket, the batsman interferes with the wicket-keeper, he shall not be out, except as provided for in law.

Batting

Batting is a technical job. A slight mistake can send batsman back to the pavilion. A bowler can commit a mistake and the maximum penalty he has to pay is to concede four or six runs. But when a batsman loses his wicket, he loses his 'life' in an innings. He can not get more chance. His techniques should be sound and his game should have a solid foundation upon which he has to build his stroke-making. Here are some points, a batsman should follow:

(i) A good grip of the bat is essential. The hands control the swing of the bat and deliver the final hit.

(ii) The way of batsman standing at the wicket, ready to face the bowler. The ideal stance is when the body-weight is evenly balanced and knees slightly for quick movement.

(iii) When the ball pitches short of length and is on the wicket the batsman must walk backward to give himself more time and room to play the shot. By walking backwards, say a couple of feat, he makes the ball relatively much shorter. The aim of the defensive shot is to keep the ball out by bringing the face of the bat square on to play the ball.

(iv) Don't look down at the back of the bat when playing the ball, otherwise the right shoulder will drop and the flight of the ball towards the bat will be lost.

(v) Don't go back with both feet pointing up the wicket, if the bat is not to come down across the line of the ball, resulting in either an edged shot to the slips or a complete miss.

(vi) Adopt the open stance when facing the inswinger, left foot pointing in the direction of extra cover.

Bowling

There are following kinds of bowling:

(i) *Full-Toss* — A ball without taking a tip on the pitch comes straight on to the batsman.

(ii) *Over-Pitch* — The ball pitching at such a length that the batsman is able to drive it without stretching his feet from the crease. Its length is more than that of the good-length delivery.

(iii) *Half-Volley* — It is that type of ball which a batsman can hit just after it has bounced.

(iv) *Swing & Swerve* — The ball can be made to swing in the air when it is delivered at fast pace, either way – into the batsman and away from him—owing to its friction with different layers of the density of air. The ball would swing more if the air is heavy with humidity.

The amount of wind, the direction it is blowing in, will also affect the movement of the ball in the air – its swing – and also the grip it is held with by the bowler.

(v) *Off-Spin* — The slow ball which after pitching turns its direction from right to left for a right-handed batsman.

(vi) *Leg-Break* — The slow ball which turns from left to right for a right-handed batsman after pitching.

(vii) *Googly* — It is an off-break ball bowled with the leg break action. It is quite difficult to bowl and is meant to deceive the batsman of its expected turn.

(viii) *Chinaman* — 'Chinaman' is the off break bowled by a left-hander with a leg-break action. You can reckon it to be a left-hander's googly ball.

(ix) *Off-Cutter* — The off-cutter is the medium fast ball which shoots from off to leg while pitching on the pitch.

(x) *Leg-Cutter* — The leg-cutter is the medium fast ball which shoots from leg to off while pitching.

(xi) Over the wicket — When a right-handed bowler bowls from the right side of the stumps.

(xii) Round the wicket — When a right-handed bowler bowls from the left side of the stumps.

Skills

Batsmen will meet the ball with a combination of defensive and attacking shots so as to hold on to their wicket while also scoring as many runs as possible. Defensive strokes play the ball safely down to the ground, away from the wicket. Attacking strokes such as the drive are used to hit the ball some distance away from the pitch to either side or straight ahead, to gain time for runs.

Bowlers have to develop their own pace and style. Most fall into two categories – fast and spin bowlers. Although there are top all-rounders, most players will specialize as bowler or batsman.

All players must be a good fielder, however—constantly on the alert, ready to retrieve and return the ball quickly or even catch it to get a batsman out. They must be able to judge in an instant which wicket is the more vulnerable and, therefore, which colleague to pass to. In some instances, a quick-thinking fielder will take aim at the wicket himself to save time if he thinks he has a chance of putting it down.

Hockey

History

All over the world, team games have evolved which require that a ball be struck or carried, and tossed at the end of a stick. Early forms of these games include hurling, shinty, bandy, pelota and hockey. Evidence shows that a crude from of stick game very much like hockey was played by Persians which travelled to Greece and later to Rome. A bar-relief found in Athens confirmed the game being played in Greece during the reign of Themistocles. The earliest mention of the present day game dates back only to 1527, when the Galway Statutes included this game in the list of prohibited games.

In 19th century the game evolved in its present form. The first Hockey Club was formed in Blackheath in 1861. During that time, the sticks were made of Oak and the end position was steamed and then pressed to give it a hooked shape. The ball was a solid cube of rubber with rounded corners. The game was standardised by the Wimbledon Hockey Club in 1883 and the first international hockey match was played between England and Ireland in 1895.

Hockey was introduced in Olympic Games in 1908. In India, this game was popularised by the British who played this game. In 1885, the first hockey club was formed in Calcutta. Later on Bombay and Punjab introduced the hockey clubs. India participated in the Olympics in 1928 at Amsterdam. Indian team won the final by defeating Holland by three goals. With this historic victory, the Indian Hockey Federation was founded. Before this in 1926, the Indian Army team went on a two-month visit to New Zealand and played 21 matches. India won 18 matches, lost one and drew 2.

The field

Hockey requires a grass or synthetic pitch, rectangular with a length of 100 yards (91.4 m) and a width of 60 yards

(54.24 m). The field shall be clearly marked out with the lines in accordance with the plan of the field. The long boundary lines are called side-lines and small boundary lines called goal-lines. All the lines must be three inches wide. The centre line and the 25-yards lines shall be marked throughout their length. To assist in the control of the hit-in across the centre-line and each 25-yards line, parallel to and 5 yards from the outer edge of side line a mark of 2 yards in length shall be marked. A mark 12 inches in length shall be placed inside the field line of play on each side-line and parallel to the goal-line and 16 yards from its inner edge. Penalty corners shall be marked inside the field of the play on the goal-lines on both sides of the goal.

Equipments

Goals : The goal posts and crossbar are white and rectangular, with a loosely fitted net. The whole structure is positioned at the centre of each back-line.

Back-Board : A back-board, 18 inches in height and 4 yards in length, shall be placed at the foot of and inside the goal nets. Side boards 18 inches in height and a minimum of 4 feet in length shall be placed at right angles to the back lines. The back-boards should be painted in dark colour.

Ball : The ball shall be of any material, usually white sewer or seamless, but of a size and weight specified may be used. The weight of the ball shall be not more than 5 ½ and 5 ¾ oz (156-163 gm) and have a circumference of 8 13/16 – 9 ¼ inches (22.4-23.5 gm). The inner portion of the ball shall be composed of cork and twine, similar to that of an ordinary cricket ball.

Stick : Idealy, the handle of the stick should reach your hips when the head is on the ground beside your feet. The hockey stick shall have a flat face on its left-hand side only. The head of the stick shall be of wood and not be edged with or have any insets or fittings of metal or any other substances nor shall there be any sharp edges or dangerous splinters. It shall have the rounded edges. The weight of the stick should be between 12 and 28 ounces (340-794 gm) and be able to pass through a 5.1 cm (interior diameter) ring. With a curved wooden head of no more than 4 inches in length (measured from the lower part of the flat face). Most adults use a stick around 90 cm long.

Flag Posts : Flag Posts must not be pointed at the top and these should be made of metal except when they are attached to a spring base. The flag posts should be more than 5 feet or less than 4 feet in height. Flags on these posts should not exceed 12 inches in width or length.

Dresses : Players of the same team must wear uniform clothing, approved by their association or club. The men should wear shirt or T-shirt with shorts and the women players should wear shirt or T-shirt with skirt. Apart from the goalkeeper, who must wear over any upper-body-protectors a shirt or garment of a different colour to the team and the opposition, plus protective clothing—full helmet, pads, hand protectors and kickers.

Shin Protection : For most of the players no special clothing is needed for hockey. However, players usually wear plastic or foam shin guards beneath their socks.

Teams

A hockey match is played between two teams of eleven players in each team. Each team including their goalkeeper is permitted to substitute any number of players during the game – substitution of players shall only take place with the permission of an umpire and during a stoppage in play other than that for award of a penalty corner or penalty stroke. After the award of a penalty corner or penalty stroke any player who is injured and has to leave the field of play can be substituted subject to the rule position.

Captain

Each team must have a captain on the field who must wear a distinctive arm-band. A captain shall indicate to the umpires any replacement captain. He should be responsible for the behaviour of all his team players.

Umpires

Two umpires are appointed to officiate the game. They both are the sole judges of fair play. Umpires shall be responsible for the decision in their half of the field. For the whole of the game, without changing ends, they shall also be responsible for ensuring that the full or agreed time of the game is played. The umpires keep a written record of goals scored and warnings/suspensions. Umpires shall blow the whistle to:

    (i)   Start and end each half of the game

    (ii)   Enforce a penalty

    (iii) Start and end a penalty stroke

    (iv) Indicate, when necessary, that the ball has passed wholly outside the field

    (v)   Signal a goal

    (vi) Re-start the game after a goal has been scored or any award

    (vii) Re-start the game after a penalty stroke in which a goal was not scored or awarded

    (viii) Stop the game for any other reason and re-start after such a stoppage.

Duration

Two periods of 35 minutes each unless otherwise agreed:

    (i)   Half time – 5 to 10 minutes as agreed: team change ends.

    (ii) Each half starts when the umpire blows the whistle for the centre pass.

To start and re-start the game

To start and re-start the game, after half time or goal, a pass-back shall be played at the centre of the field. The pass-back for the start of the game shall be made by a player of the team which opts for the start of the game. The pass-back shall be taken by a player of the opposing team after the half time and after a goal by a player of the opposing team shall be within 5 yards of the ball and all players must be in their own half of the field. If the striker hits at but misses the ball, the pass-back shall be retaken. The player taking the pass-back shall not play the ball second time until it is played or touched by another player.

Centre Pass : This will be played from the centre of the field. A push or hit may be played in any direction; all the players other than the player making the pass shall be in their half of the field. This will be made at the start of the game, by a player of the team which did not choose ends. After a goal, by a player of the team against which the goal was scored or awarded:

Bully : The game shall be re-started with a bully when:

(i)   The ball in play has to be replaced.

(ii)   There is a simultaneous breach of the rules by both the teams.

(iii)   The ball is lodged in a goalkeeper's pad or player's or umpire's clothing.

(iv)   When time has been stopped for injury or any other reason and there has been no offence.

Ball outside the field : When the ball passes completely over the side-line or back-line it shall be out of play and it or another ball shall be used to re-start the play. The player playing the ball is not required to be wholly inside or outside the side line.

Scoring a goal:

(i)   A goal is scored when the ball is played in the circle by an attacker and does not go outside the circle before passing completely over the goal-line and under the crossbar.

(ii)   The ball may be played by or touch the stick or body of a defender before or after being played in the circle by an attacker.

(iii)   After a stoppage of play inside the circle, the ball must again be played from inside the circle by an attacker before a goal can be scored.

(iv)   A goal shall be awarded if a goalkeeper breaches the penalty stroke rules preventing a goal being scored.

(v)   The team scoring the greater number of goals shall be the winner.

Offside:

Players are in an offside position if, at the moment the ball is passed or played to them by a player of their team, they are in front of the ball and nearer the back-line than two opponents or in their opponents' 25-yard area.

Payers so positioned are not committing an offence unless the ball is passed to them or they gain an advantage for their team. Players level with second defender are not outside. Players off the field near to the 25-yards area or behind their opponents' back-line can be in offside position.

Conduct of play

Hockey can be a dangerous game unless it is played with consideration for others. This rule prohibits or explains actions which affect the safety of all players. Players should not play the ball intentionally with the back of the stick, they should not take part in or interfere with the game unless they have their stick in their hand. They should not play the ball dangerously or in such a way as to be likely to lead to dangerous play. A ball is dangerous when it causes legitimate evasive action by players. The players should also not throw any object or piece of playing equipment on to the field, at the ball, at another player or at an umpire. Goalkeeper must not waste time when ball is inside their own circle.

Penalties

The penalty incurred by an infringement of the rules depends on where it occurred and now serious it was. Generally, the penalty is a free hit to the opposition, but if, for example, a defender inside his own circle intentionally prevents a goal from being scored, the opposition will be awarded a penalty stroke. Another penalty is the penalty corner – for unintentional offences inside the defender's own circle, or for intentional offences within their own 25 yards area, but outside the circle. Goals can not be scored directly from a penalty corner. The ball must be completely stopped outside the circle before the strike; a direct strike must hit the goal back-board while an indirect strike does not need to.

Free hit

More than 5 yards from the circle : Close to where the offence occurred. 'Close to' allows the free hit to be taken within playing distance of where the offence occurred. It is intended that no undue advantage be gained but the flow of the game maintained.

Outside the circle : To the defence within 16 yards of the back-line upto 16 yards from the back-line in line with the offence, parallel to the side-line.

Inside the circle: To the defence anywhere within the circle or outside it up to 16 yards from the back-line in line with the offence, parallel to the side-line.

Within 5 yards of the circle to the attack : Close to where the offence occurred all players of both teams other than the taker to be at least 5 yards from the ball.

After playing the ball the striker must not play the ball again or approach within playing distance of it until it has been played by another player. If a player is standing within 5 yards of the ball in order to gain an advantage, the free hit need not be delayed.

Penalty corner

It is awarded when a defender deliberately plays the ball over his back line, commits offence as within the circle or within 25 yards line after an intentional foul or after an infringement at a corner.

While taking the penalty corner the rest of the players of the attacking team are required to be outside the circle. A maximum number of 5 players of opposing team are permitted to stand behind their own goal line and all other players should be beyond the centre-line. The penalty corner is taken at least 10 yards from the goalpost on the goal line. No shot at goal shall be played until the ball be stopped or come to rest on the ground outside the circle.

Penalty stroke

A penalty stroke is awarded to the opposing team if that team has possession or the opportunity to gain possession of the ball in the circle and in the umpire's opinion. The penalty stroke shall be push, flick or scoop stroke taken from the spot 7 yards in front of the centre of the goal by a player of the attacking team and defended by the goalkeeper of the opposing team on the field at the time the breach occurred. The attacking player shall not take the penalty stroke until the umpire, having satisfied himself that both defender and attacker are ready, was indicated that he shall do so by blowing his whistle. The goalkeeper shall stand on the goal-line after the attacker taking the stroke and the goalkeeper are in position and the umpire has blown the whistle, the goalkeeper shall not leave the goal-line or move either of his feet until the ball has been played.

Injuries/Accidents:

If a goal is scored before the game is stopped it shall be allowed if it would have been scored had the accident not occurred.

If a player is incapacitated, the umpire may stop the game.

An injury or bleeding player should leave the field as soon as it is safe to do so and receive treatment off the field unless medical reasons prevent this.

Players shall not return to the field until their wounds have been dressed and no player remain on, enter or re-enter the field wearing blood-stained clothing.

If an umpire is incapacitated, the game shall be stopped; if injured player cannot continue, he should be replaced.

The game shall be restarted with a bully, with the appropriate penalty or with a centre pass if a goal is scored.

Skills

Players in a team are allocated to one of four positions:
(i)   Forward
(ii) Midfielder
(iii) Defender
(iv) Goalkeeper

Although these roles are flexible enough to meet the demands of whatever team strategy is chosen. All players require stick control and co-ordination to be able to receive the ball, bring it under control and then pass or dribble it quickly and accurately. Forwards must be able to shoot well and quickly to take advantage of any opportunity to score. Midfielders are very much team players, supporting both the attack and the defence as needed. They must constantly be aware of other players' positions throughout the field. Defenders remain largely towards the back or the end of the field. Marking and tackling are the basic elements of defensive play. The goalkeeper requires particular skills of his own. Any part of the body or the stick may be used to stop the ball, so this player needs to be extremely agile, quick and to have a high level of concentration at all the time.

Football

History

Football has a long history and it is recorded that this game was played in China during 300 B.C. It was known by the name of 'Tsu Chu' which means "to kick the leather ball with the feet." In medieval Europe, street football was banned as a menace to the public. But it became formalized in 1863 with the foundation of the Football Association which drew up a set of rules to co-ordinate the way it was played. The game founded on these rules – now known as Association of Football, Soccer or just plain football – is today the most popular game in the world as well as the most popular spectator sport.

The first international football match was played between England and Scotland. In 1904 delegates from seven countries met and they founded the Federation International de Football Association (FIFA). First world championship was organized by FIFA in 1930 at Montevideo and the Olympic champion Uraguay lifted the Jules-Rimet Trophy.

Football came to India with the British. Some British soldiers used to play this game during the freedom movement in India. Indians took much interest and soon the game was very popular. Indian team took part in Olympics in 1948. India made a spectacular record by winning the first Asian Games title held in New Delhi in 1951.

The field

Football field must be rectangular and traditionally with a grass surface. The length of the field must be between 100-130 yards and the width must be between 50-100 yards. The field should be divided into two equal parts. A circle with 10 yards radius shall be marked in the centre of the field. The field shall be marked with distinctive lines, not more than 5 inches in width. A flag on a post not less than 5 ft high shall be placed at each corner. A similar flag-post may be placed opposite the halfway-line on each side of the field. Two lines at a distance of 6 yards from each goal-post shall be marked at each end and shall join each other by a line drawn parallel with the goal line. The inside area of these lines is called goal area. Two lines at a distance of 18 yards from goal line shall be marked and joined by a line marked parallel to goal line. This area is called the penalty area.

Equipments

Ball : The ball shall be spherical with an outer casing of leather or approved substitute material. The inner part (bladder) shall be of rubber. The circumference of the ball must be 27-28 inches and it must weigh between 14-16 oz (410-450 gm). The pressure shall be equal to 0.6-1.1 atmospheres which equals 600-1, $10092/cm^2$ at sea level.

Goalpost : The goalposts are made of wood, steel or any other approved material. These are placed on the centre of the goal line. Two upright posts 7.32 m (24 ft.) apart are placed at equal distance from the corner flags and joined by a horizontal crossbar of 8 ft.

Clothing : Jersy or shirt, shorts, stockings, shinguards and footwear are the basic equipments of a player. A player shall not wear anything which is dangerous to another player.

Shinguard must be covered entirely by the stockings, shall be made of a suitable material and shall afford a reasonable degree of protection. The goalkeeper shall wear different colours from his team which distinguish him from the other players. He should also use the leather or cotton gloves to protect his fingers. The bars of the shoe shall be made of leather or rubber. The studs are of both replaceable and non-replaceable and should be round in plan and minimum ½ inch in diameter.

Teams

Football match is played between two teams. Each team is consisting of 11 players including one goalkeeper. There are two substitute players in each team who can enter the game subject to some conditions:

— That the authority of the international association(s) or national association(s) concerned, has been obtained.

— That substitutes are used, as allowed in the rules of the match.

— More than two substitute are not allowed in any match and their names are required to be given to referee prior to the commencement of the match.

— Substitute may be used in any other match, if agreed by the two teams concerned and intimated to the referee, before the match.

— After the replacement of substitute player the referee shall be informed of the proposed substitution; before it is made, the substitute shall not enter the field of play until the player he is replacing has left and then only, after having a signal from the referee, he shall enter the field during a stoppage in the game, and at the half way line, a player who has been replaced shall not take any further part in the game, a substitute shall be subject to the authority and jurisdiction of the referee whether called upon to play or not and the substitution is completed when the substitute enters the field of play, from which moment he became a player and the player whom he is replacing ceases to be a player.

Officials

Referee : A referee shall be appointed to officiate in the game. His powers and authorities granted to him by the laws of the game commence as soon as he enters the field. His decisions on points of fact connected with the play shall be final so far as the result of the game is concerned. He is also given two assistants (linesmen) as helping hand. He shall:

(i)   Enforce the laws and decide any disputed point;

(ii)   Will hold the decision, if he feels that by giving a penalty there shall be undue advantage to a team;

(iii)   Works like a time-keeper and record-keeper. He may also allow the full or agreed upon time, adding there to all time lost through accident or such type of cause;

(iv)   Have authority to caution any player who is guilty of misconduct or unreasonable behaviour and, if he persists, the referee may suspend him;

(v)   Send off the field any player(s) who, in his opinion, is guilty of violent conduct. Serious foul play or use of foul and abusive language;

(vi)   Allow no person other than the player and linesman to enter the field without his permission;

(vii)   Signal for recommencement of the game after all stoppages;

(viii) Decides that the ball provided for the game meets all the requirements as per law.

Linesman : Two linesmen shall be appointed who act under the supervision of the referee. Their duties are to indicate that the ball is out of field and from where, which team is entitled for corner-kick, goal-kick or throw-in, requirement of substitute player in the field etc. The linesmen should be equipped with flags by the club/trust/board. Referee can change any linesman by calling a substitute linesman.

Duration

A game lasts 90 minutes and is divided into two halves of 45 minutes each, with teams changing ends at half-time. (For cup matches this may be extended by another 30 minutes of 'extra time' in the case of a draw.) The half time interval shall not exceed 15 minutes. Competition rules shall clearly stipulate the duration of the half-time interval. The duration of the half-time interval may be altered only with the consent of the referee.

Starting of match

A football match is started after the choice of the ends and the kick-off shall be decided by the toss of a coin. Winning

Rules of Various Sports

team shall have the option of choice of ends or the kick-off. The game shall be started by a player taking a place kick. The kicker shall not play the ball second time until it has been touched or played by another player.

After a goal has been scored, the game shall be restarted in like manner by a player of the team losing the goal.

After the half-time : When restarting after the half-time, ends shall be changed and the kick-off shall be taken by a player of the opposite team to that of the player who started the game.

Goal

Once the game has started, no player(s), except the goal-keeper(s) within their own penalty areas, may intentionally handle the ball. By kicking or heading it the players of one team seek to move the ball from another until one of their side is in a position to shoot the ball into the goal of the opposite side with his foot or head. The law relating to the method of scoring reads: "A goal is scored when the whole ball has passed over the goal line, between the goalposts and under the crossbar, provided, it has not been thrown, carried or propelled by hand or arm, by a player of the attacking side, except in the case of a goalkeeper, who is within his penalty area. The winning side is that which gets the ball more frequently into the opposing goal."

Scoring:

Except as otherwise provided by these laws, a goal is scored when the whole of the ball has passed over the goal line, between the goalposts and under the crossbar. The team scoring the maximum goals is the winner. If no goals, or an equal number of goals are scored, the game shall be termed a 'draw'. The result is declared by the scoring points. For example team A scored 3 goals and team B scored 1 goal, the result will be declared as team A won by 3-1 goals.

Ball in and out of play

The ball is out of play:

(i)   When it has wholly crossed the goal line or touchline, whether on the ground or in the air.

(ii) When the game has been stopped by the referee for some reasons.

The ball is in the play at all other times from the start of the match to the finish including:

(i) If it rebounds from a goalpost, crossbar or corner flag-post into the field of the play.

(ii) If it rebounds off either the referee or assistant referees (linesmen) when they are in the field of play.

(iii) In the event of a supposed infringement of the laws, until a decision is given.

Offside

A player is in an offside position if he is near to his opponent's goal line than ball, unless:

(i) He is in his own half of the field of play.

(ii) He is not nearer to his opponent's goal line than at least two of his opponents.

It is not an offence in itself to be in an offside position. A player shall only be penalized for being in an offside position if, at the moment the ball touches, or is played by one of his team he is, in the opinion of the referee, involved in activity play by:

(i) Interfacing with play

(ii) Interfacing with an opponent

(iii) Gaining an advantage by being in that position.

A players shall not be declared offside by the referee –

(i) Merely because of his being in an offside position

(ii) If he receives the ball direct from a goal-kick, a corner-kick or a throw-in.

When any of the player is declared offside the referee shall award an indirect free kick, which shall be taken by a player of opposite team from the place where the infringement occurred, unless the offence is committed by a player in his opponent's goal area, in which case the free kick shall be taken from any point within the goal area.

Offences

If a player commits a major physical offence such as kicking, striking or pushing an opponent, a direct free kick is awarded to the opposing team. This also applies if the ball is deliberately handled by any player other than the goalkeeper.

Other offences such as time-wasting or indulging in dangerous play are penalized with an indirect free kick for the other team. For any free kick, the kicker's opponents must keep a distance of 10 yards, between themselves and the ball.

A player who argues with the referee or persistently breaks the rules will be shown the yellow card (an official caution), while more serious conduct such as violent behaviour or foul language will result in the player being sent immediately off the field.

Free-kick

There are two types of free kicks indicated in the game – direct and indirect. Direct free kick means from which a goal can be scored direct against the offending side and indirect means from which a goal cannot be scored unless the ball has been played or touched by a player other than the kicker before passing through the goal. When a player is taking direct or indirect free kick outside his own penalty area, all of the opposing players shall be at least 10 yards from the ball, until it is in play. If a player is taking direct or indirect free kick inside his own penalty area, all of the opposing players shall be at least 10 yards from the ball and shall remain outside the penalty area until the ball has been kicked out of the area.

Notwithstanding any other reference in these laws to the point from which a free kick is to be taken:

(i) Any free kick awarded to the defending team, within its own goal area, may be taken from any point within the goal area.

(ii) Any indirect free kick awarded to the attacking team within its opponent's goal area shall be taken from the part of the goal-area line which runs parallel to the goal line at the point nearest to where the offence was committed.

Punishment : A player (who has taken the free kick) after taking the free kick, if he plays the ball a second time before it has been touched or played by another player an indirect free kick shall be taken by a player of the opposing team from the spot where the infringement occurred, unless the offence is committed by a player in his opponent's goal area in which case the free kick shall be taken from any point within the goal area.

Penalty kick

A penalty kick shall be taken from the penalty mark and, when it is being taken, all players with the exception of the player taking the kick, properly identified and the opposing goalkeeper shall be within the field of play but outside the penalty area (at least 10 yards from the penalty mark) and must stand behind the penalty mark.

The opposing goalkeeper must stand without moving the feet on his own goal line, between the goal posts, until the ball is kicked. The player taking the penalty kick should not play the ball second time until it has been touched or played by another player. The ball shall be deemed in play directly if it is kicked i.e. when it has travelled the distance of its circumference. A goal may be scored by a penalty kick.

Punishment : For any infringement of this law:

By defending team, the kick shall be retaken if a goal has not resulted; by the attacking team other than by the player taking the kick, if a goal is scored it shall be disallowed and the kick retaken; by the player taking the committed after the ball is in play, a player of the opposing team shall take an indirect free kick from the spot where the infringement occurred subject to the overriding conditions imposed in law.

Throw-in

While playing the game, when the whole of the ball passes over the touchline, either on the ground or in the air, it shall be throw-in from the point where it crossed the line, in any direction by a player of the team opposite to that of the player who last touched it. The thrower at the moment of delivering the ball must face the field of play and part of each foot shall be either on the touchline or on the ground outside the touchline.

The thrower shall use both hands and shall deliver the ball from behind and over his head. The ball shall be in play immediately as it enters the field of play, but the thrower shall not again play the ball until it has been touched or played by another player. A goal shall not be scored direct from a throw-in.

Punishment : If the ball is improperly thrown in, the throw-in shall be taken by a player of the opposing team. If the thrower plays the ball a second time before it has been touched or played by another player, an indirect free kick shall be taken by a player of the opposing team from the place where the infringement occurred subject to the overriding conditions imposed in the law.

Goal kick

During the game when the whole of the ball passes over the goal line excluding that portion between the goalposts, either in the air or on the ground, having last been played by one of the attacking team, it shall be kicked direct into play beyond the penalty area from any point within the goal area, by a player of the defending team. A goalkeeper shall not receive the ball into his hands from a goal kick in order that he may thereafter kick it into play. The kicker shall not play the ball second time until it has been touched or played by another player. A goal shall not be scored direct from such a kick.

Punishment : A player who is taking the goal kick, if he plays the ball second time after it has passed beyond the penalty-area, but before it has touched or been played by another player, an indirect free kick shall be awarded to the opposing team.

Corner kick

When the ball passes over the goal line, excluding that portion between the goalposts, either in the air or on the ground, having last played by one of the defending team, a player of the attacking team shall take a corner kick i.e. the whole of the ball shall be placed within the quarter circle at the nearest corner flag-post, which must not be moved, and it shall be kicked from that position. A goal may be scored from such a kick.

Punishment : If the player, who has taken the corner kick, plays the ball a second time before it has been touched or played by another player, the referee shall award an indirect free-kick to opposing team. For any other infringement the kick shall be taken again.

Skills

Although all players require stamina, speed and the ability to control a ball, particular qualities are desirable for each for the four play positions.

Defenders must be skilled at tackling and heading. Midfield players need the stamina to keep up with play at all times and the flexibility to play defence or attack as required. Strikers need to be especially skilful with the ball and good at heading. They also need to be able to respond quickly and accurately to good opportunities. Goalkeeper must have the ability and reflexes to be able to block balls coming in from all kinds of angles. They also need a high level of concentration and good judgement.

Above are the listed basic rules of association of football. However, these rules are continually modified year after year by additional rulings called international board decisions.

Volleyball

History

Volleyball can be played indoors and outdoors. From its humble beginning in 1895, this has become a popular sport worldwide. It can be played as an informal, recreational game or highly competitive, vigorous one at competition level.

William G. Morgan is known to be the inventor of volleyball. He was a physical training instructor at Y.M.C.A. in Holyoke. During the starting days, it was played with the bladder of a football. Dr. Hollstead of Springfield College named it as 'Volleyball'. Before this it was known by the name of 'Minonette'. It was said that this game was devised for those people who were not fit enough to play basketball.

During the World War I and II, it was popular among U.S. Servicemen, who helped to make it an international sport. The International Association of Volleyball was formed in 1947 and later on in 1954 it was introduced in 'Pan American Games'. Volleyball was included in Olympic Games in 1964 Tokyo Olympics.

In India the first volleyball match was played at the Y.M.C.A. College of Madras. India played its first match in 1936 during the All Hindi Volleyball Championship in Lahore. The match was won by the team of Punjab and in respect of this victory, the Volleyball Federation of India was established in Ludhiana (Punjab).

The court

The playing court is a rectangle measuring 18 x 9 metres surrounded by a rectangular free zone of minimum of 2 metres and with a space free from any obstructions to a height of a minimum surface. The court should be flat and uniform. Only wooden or synthetic surfaces are allowed for international competitions. The centre line divides the court in two parts. Each part is then divided into front and back zone by the attack line. All lines in the court shall be marked 5 cm wide and of different colour from the playing surface. Lighting on a court should be 500 to 1500 lux measured one metre high from the playing surface.

Beach volleyball is a separate game which is played at Olympics using a sand court of the same dimensions.

Equipments

Net: The net is a mesh one metre wide and 9.50 metre long vertically placed over the axis of the centre line. The net shall be made of 10 cm square dark stitched mesh, with two folds of white canvas 10 cm wide; each 5 cm fold sewn along the full length of the top of the net and a flexible cable stretched through to keep the top of the net tense.

Posts : Two rounded posts preferably adjustable and smooth with a height of 2.55 metre (8 ft.) support the net one at each end. The posts must be fixed to the ground at a distance of between 0.50 and 1.00 metre from each side line.

Antennae : Two flexible vertical antennae are fastened at the outer edge of each side band to mark the boundaries that the ball must keep to when crossing the net. The antennas are made with fibreglass or similar material. They shall be 1.80 metre long 10 mm in diameter. They are considered as parts of the net and mark its side lines.

Ball : The ball shall be made of a flexible leather case containing a bladder made of rubber or similar material. The ball shall be spherical with a circumference of 65-67 cm. The weight of the ball must not be less than 260 gm and not exceed more than 280 gm. The inside pressure of the ball must be of 0.30 – 0.325 kg/sq. cm. The colour of the ball must be light and uniform.

Players/Teams

A volleyball match is played between two teams. Each team consists of a maximum of 12 players (including 6 substitutes) one coach, one assistant coach and one doctor. Only the players recorded on the score-sheet may participate in the match. Once the team captain and coach have signed the score-sheet, the recorded players cannot be changed. Captain will be appointed from amongst those of the team players. The coach and the captain himself can designate another player to act as a game captain in case of substitution of captain.

Dress

All the players required to wear jersey, shorts and shoes. It must be uniform, clean and of the same colour for the team. Players' shirts must be numbered on front and back (1 to 18).

Warming up

All the players will have to warm up for 3 minutes at the net, before the starting of the game. If both captains ask to warmup at the same time both teams may be at the net for 6 or 10 minutes each. In the event of consecutive warm-ups, the team that has won the right to serve takes the first turn at the net.

Game

Before starting the match, the referee carries out a toss up in the presence of both captains. The winner of the toss chooses the court or the right to serve first. All the players except the server must be in their own court at the moment the ball is served, with each team arranged in two rows of three players – three front row players and three back row players behind them. The ball is served by a player of the serving team. He stands behind the end line. He hits the ball with one hand or arm, after which players are free to move about within their own court.

Score

A match is won by a team who wins 3 sets. In the case of 2-2 tie, the deciding set is played as a tie-breaker with the rally-point system. The scoring system in four sets differs from that of the decisive set. A set is won by a team who first scores 15 points with a minimum lead of 2 points. If any team fails to serve or return the ball or commits any mistake, the opposing team wins a point or service. Rally point system is used in the decisive set in which case no point limit is put at 17 and the game continues until a score with two points difference is achieved. In the first four sets maximum points which can be won by a team can be 17. The 17th point wins the set with only a one-point lead. If, after receiving a warning from the first referee, a team refuses to play it is declared in default and the opposing team is given by default the score of 15 – 0 for each set and 3 – 0 for the match.

Positions

(i)   When the ball is hit by the server, both the players of the teams must be within their court in two rows of three players. These rows may be broken at the starting of the game.

(ii) The 3 players along the net are front-row players and the other 3 players are back-row players. Each back-row player must be positioned further back from the centre line than the corresponding front-row players.

(iii) Players' positions are determined and controlled according to the positions of their feet contacting the ground. Each front-row player must have at least part of one foot closer to the centre line than the feet of the corresponding back-row players. Each right side player must have at least part of one foot closer to the right side line than the feet of the centre player in the same row.

(iv) After serving the ball, the players may move around and occupy any position on their own court and in the free zone.

Rotation

(i)   The rotation order as recorded on the score sheet at the beginning of each set must remain same throughout the set.

(ii) When the team receiving the serve wins the rally or the opponent commits any fault, it wins the right to serve and its players must rotate one position clockwise.

(iii) A different rotation order for each new set may be used by the team and any player recorded on the score sheet may be registered in the new starting line-up.

Ball 'in' and 'out' of play

The first referee's whistle authorizes the service—the ball is 'in' play from the hit of the service. The ball is 'in' when it touches the floor of the playing court including the boundary lines.

The rally ends with the referee's whistle. However, if the whistle is due to a fault made in play, the ball is 'out' of play the moment the fault was committed: The part of the ball contacts the floor is completely outside the boundary lines, it touches an object outside the court, the ceiling or a person out of play, if touches the antennae, ropes, posts, net itself outside the antennae/side bands, it crosses completely underneath the vertical plane of the net.

Assisted hit

Any of the player is not permitted to take support from a teammate or any structure or object in order to reach the ball within the playing area. However, the player who is about to commit fault may be stopped or held back by a team-mate.

Ball at the net

The ball sent to the opponent's court must go over the net within the crossing space. The crossing space is the part of the vertical plane of the net limited as follows:

Below, by the top of the net, at the sides, by the antennae and their imaginary extension and above by the ceiling.

The ball has crossed the net plane to the opponent's free zone totally or partly outside of the crossing space, may be played back within the team hits provided that the opponent's court is not touched by the player and the ball when played back crosses the net plane again outside the crossing space on the same side of the court. The opposing team may not prevent such action.

The ball is completely 'out' when it crosses the lower space under the net.

When crossing the net the ball may touch it, except during the service. A ball driven into the net may be recovered within the limits of the three team hits. If the ball rips the mesh of the net or tears it down, the rally is cancelled and game will start again.

Player at the net

Every team must play within its own playing area and space. The ball may, however, be retrieved from beyond the free zone. A player is permitted to pass a hand beyond the net after an attack hit provided that the contact has been made within the player's own playing space. It is permitted to penetrate into the opponent's space under the net, provided that does not interfere with the opponent's play. Following are the faults of players at the net:

(*i*)   If he penetrates into the opponent's space under the net interfering with the latter's play.

(*ii*) If he touches the ball in opponent's space before or during the opponent's attack hit.

(*iii*) It he penetrates into the opponent's court.

(*iv*) If a player touches the net.

Blocking

It is an action of players close to the net to intercept the ball coming from the opponents by reaching higher than the top of the net. A collective block is executed by two or three players close to each other and is completed when one of them touches the ball. A block contact is not counted as a team hit in blocking, the players may place hands and arms beyond the net, provided that the action does not interfere with the opponent's play. Thus it is permitted to touch the ball beyond the net until the opponent has executed an attack hit.

Blocking faults:

(i)   The blocker touches the ball in the opponent's space either before or simultaneously with the opponent's action.

(ii) A back-row player completes a block or participates in a complete one.

(iii) A player blocks the ball in the opponent's space from outside the antennae.

(iv) The ball is sent 'out' off the block.

(v)   A player blocks the opponent's service.

Interruptions

During time-out the players must go to the free zone near

their bench. The reserve players should also leave the warming-up area and go to the bench. After time-out is granted, the second referee checks the time and whether the teams are near or on the bench. During time-out, reserve players may warm up in the free-zone without the ball. A request for substitution before the start of a set is permitted and should be recorded as a regular game interruption in that set. One or two time-outs and one request for player substitution by either team may follow one another with no need to resume the game. A team is not authorized to request consecutive interruptions for player substitutions unless the game has been resumed. However, two or more players may be substituted during the same interruption.

Change of courts

After each set, the teams change the sides of their courts with the exception of the deciding set. Other team members change their benches in the deciding set. Once a team reaches eight points, the teams change courts without delay and the players' positions remain the same if the change is not made at the proper time. It will take place as soon as the error is noticed. The score at the time that the change is made remains the same.

Misconduct

In case of un-sportsmanlike conduct a warning is issued to the defaulter and so recorded on the score-sheet. In case of rude conduct, the team is penalized with the loss of a rally which is recorded on the score-sheet. Repeated rude conduct is sanctioned by expulsion. The referee must show the yellow and red cards together to the person sanctioned. The team member who is sanctioned with expulsion must leave the playing area, the bench and the warm-up area for the rest of the set. Expulsion is valid for one set only. The second expulsion of the same team member is regarded as a disqualification.

For any offensive conduct and aggression, towards the refereeing corps, opponents, teammates or spectators, the player must leave the playing area, the bench and the warm-up area, immediately. This is signalled by the first referee by showing the yellow and red cards seperatively to the player at fault. Any misconduct occurring before or between the sets is sanctioned according to rules and apply in the same set.

Skills

The serve – a potentially dynamic start to a rally. The most basic is an underarm serve, although experienced players use a serve similar to that performed with a racket in tennis or the jump serve – used at the top level of play, in which a server throws the ball both up and then runs to meet it, hitting it as he jumps into the air. The standard procedure for receiving and returning the ball is the dig-set-smash approach. The three hits permitted to a team are used to absorb the speed of a serve, pass it and then smash it to return it over the net, hopefully to score a point.

Basketball

History

Basketball is called an American game because it had its origin in the Y.M.C.A. Institution in U.S. and it grew in an American environment. The credit for starting this game and framing its rules goes to an experienced person, Dr. James A. Naismith. He was a member of the faculty in Springfield College, Massachusetts. During the winter of 1891-92, he was looking for a vigorous indoor game which could be used to stimulate interest among students. He nailed two peach baskets on the walls of his gymnasium and formed two teams to play the game. A soccer ball was thrown up and the participants tried their tricks to toss the ball into the peach baskets.

The peach baskets were replaced in 1906 by hoops fixed on a pole or board 10 ft above the ground. Several other changes were introduced by members and supporters of the game and basketball was standardized to some extent. Through many years of refinement and development, basketball has evolved into a major sport which is highly organized and specialized.

The first rule book was published by the Y.M.C.A. College of Physical Education, Springfield, USA in 1895. The international association for this game was formed in 1932 by the name of 'Federation International de Basketball Association' (FIBA). In 1936, the game was first included in Berlin Olympic Games.

In India, basketball was played firstly in 1930. The first Indian National Championship was conducted in 1934 in New Delhi. In 1950, the Basketball Federation of India was formed. Its popularity stems from the fact that it is a fast-scoring game in which there is intense activity from the beginning till end. In recent years women from many countries including India have taken keen interest in playing this game.

The court

The playing field of basketball is known as court. The court shall be rectangular, of hard surface and free from obstructions. It must have the dimensions of 28 metres in length and 15 metres in width. The height of the ceiling should be at least 7 metres. The playing surface should be uniformly and adequately lighted. The court shall be marked by well-defined lines at every point at least 2 metres from any obstructions. The lines are marking out the boundaries, centre line and circle line. The centre cricle shall have a radius of 1.80 metre. The radius shall be measured to the outer edge of the circumference. All lines should be 5 cm wide and drawn in the same colour.

Equipments

Ball : The ball shall be made with rubber bladder covered with a case of leather, rubber or synthetic material. It should be spherical and consist of a circumference of 74.9-78 cm (appx-30 inch). The ball must weigh between 567 gm – 650 gm (20-23 oz) and when dropped on the playing surface from a height of 1.80 metre it must rebound to a height of 1.20-1.40 metre approximately.

Backboards : Two rectangular backboards shall be fixed at each end of the court. The backboards should be made of 0.03 m (appx-1 inch) wooden hard board or transparent material: 1.80 metre wide and 1.05 metre high with the lower edges 2.90 metre from the floor. Both backboards shall be firmly mounted in a position at each end. Their centres shall lie in the perpendiculars erected at the points on the court 1.20 metre from the inner edge of mid point of each end line. Backboard should be of a bright colour in contrast with the background.

Baskets : A basket is attached to each backboard. The ring of the basket is made of solid iron, painted orange with the inside diameter of 0.45 metre. The net is made of white cord and is suspended from the ring. It is 40-45 cm long and constructed so that it checks the ball momentarily as it passes through.

Technical equipment

A game clock to time periods of play, a stop-watch to time

time-outs, a 30-second device (automatic, digital, indicating time in seconds) for the administration of the 30- second rule; very loud signals for the time-keeper/scorer and 30-second operator.

Players

There shall be 10 players in a team including one captain and 5 substitute players. Five players from each team shall be on the court during playing time and may be substituted within the provisions contained in the rules. There should be one coach who may be assisted by an assistant coach. Each player shall be numbered on the front and back of his shirt with plain numbers of solid colour contrasting with the colour of the shirt. The uniform of the players shall consist of shirt, shorts of the same dominant colour contrasting with the opposing team, whereby the shorts may be of a different colour from the shirts. The players shall also wear socks and shoes.

Officials

A referee and an umpire, assisted by a time-keeper, a scorer, assistant scorer and a 30-second operator shall be appointed for a match. All officials must wear their prescribed uniform and are required to conduct the game in accordance with the rules. This includes putting the ball in play, determining when the ball becomes dead etc. Blowing the whistle to stop action after the ball has become dead, administrating penalties, ordering time-out, handing ball to a player when such player is to make a throw-in from out-of-bounds whenever this is provided for in the rules and silently counting seconds.

The game

Referee steps into the centre circle of the court with the ball and starts the game. Two opposing players take their places in the circle. The referee tosses the ball up into the air between them and once it begins its descent, both players attempt to tap it to their team members. The game clock starts when the ball is tapped the first time, and until such time all other players must remain outside the centre circle. a goal is scored when the ball enters the basket from above and remains within or passes through. The team scoring the maximum number of goals wins the game.

Duration

A game consists of two halves of 20 minutes each with an interval of 10 minutes. If the score is tied, play continues for as many extra 5-minute periods as necessary to break the tie. The time of interval may be increased depending upon the local conditions.

Throw-in

Any opponent of the team credited with the score shall be entitled to throw the ball in from any point out-of-bounds on or behind the endline at the end of the court where the goal was made. He may pass the ball to his teammate or behind the endline, but the five-second count starts the instant the ball is at the disposal of the first player out-of-bounds. The official should not handle the ball unless by doing so the game can be resumed more quickly. The player who is throwing the ball in shall stand out-of-bounds as designated by the official, at the place nearest to the point of the infraction or where the game was stopped. A player throwing the ball should not touch the ball in the court before it has been touched by another player. He should stop on the court while releasing the ball.

Forfeit

A team shall lose the game by forfeit if:
(i)   It refuses to play after being instructed to do so by the referee.
(ii)   By this action it prevents the game from being played.
(iii)   15 minutes after starting time, the team is not present or is not able to field five players.

Penalty : The game shall be awarded to the opposing team and the score shall be 20-0. The forfeiting team shall receive zero points in the classification.

Dribbling

This is the act of bouncing the ball on the floor continuously and moving along with it. The ball is bounced and controlled by one hand or by the left and right hands alternatively. Dribbling is done by smoothly pushing the ball with the fingers. If the palm of the hand is used, it will result in a sort of slapping action and, therefore, the ball should not be hit by the palm when dribbling. There are two types of dribbling –
— High dribble
— Low dribble

The high dribble is used when a player wants to move fast with the ball. He keeps the body in normal position. In the low dribbling the ball is kept quite low, between the knees and waist. Thus the dribbler crouches to a convenient position. This is an effective way of guarding the ball particulary when the opponents are fairly near.

Shooting

Scoring points by shooting the ball through the ring is the primary objective in basketball. All the other offensive fundamentals such as passing, catching, dribbling and foot-work represent only the preparatory part of shooting. A player should be proficient in the art of shooting. There are two ways to getting the ball through the ring:

(i) The ball is put directly into the basket and it goes through without touching the board or the ring.

(ii) The ball is thrown on the board and it rebounds into the basket. As a general rule the second method is adopted when the player is at a convenient angle and the ball rebounds off the board at about 45°. This implies that the board is not used when the shooter is at the centre and extreme sides. However it is a matter of individual preference and, therefore, no hard and fast rule could be laid down.

Dead ball

The ball becomes dead when:

(i) It is apparent that the ball will not go into the basket, on a free throw for a technical foul by the coach, assistant coach, substitute or team follower.

(ii)   An official's whistle is blown while the ball is alive or in the play.

(iii)   Time expires for a half or an extra period.

(iv)   Any goal has been made.

(v)   The ball already in flight on a shot for goal is touched by a player of either team after time has expired for a half or extra period, or after a foul has been called.

(vi)   The 30-second operator's signal is sounded while the ball is alive.

3-Second rule

A player shall not remain more than 3 seconds in the restricted area between his opponent's end line and free-throw line while the ball is in control of his team. The lines bounding the restricted area are part of the restricted area and a player touching one of these lines is in the area. The three-second restriction is in force in all out-of-bounds situations. The count shall start at the moment the player making the throw-in is out of bounds and the ball is at his disposal. The 3-second restriction does not apply when:

— The ball is dead
— The ball is in the air during a shot for goal
— The ball is rebounding from the backboard

10-Second rule

If any team has possessioned the ball in its back court, it must move into the front court within 10 seconds. The ball goes into a team's front court when it touches the court beyond the centre lines or touches a player of that team who has part of his body in contact with the court beyond the centre line.

Pivoting

A player who is stationary may step in any direction, any number of times with one foot, keeping the other in the same place. This act is known as pivoting. It may be done to the rear or the sides or forward. The rear pivot is performed by lifting the left foot and moving it back in an arc. The same may be done by shifting the right foot also, and in this case the player will face a different direction. The technique of the

Rules of Various Sports

front pivot is same as the rear pivot.

Catching

Catching refers to receiving the ball well as to keep it under control. Before making the catch, the arms and the hands are extended slightly towards the ball and are withdrawn as it is received. The ball should be held with the fingers spread out and the palms are not generally used. The person who passes the ball also has to play a good part. He should pass the ball in proper manner. There are following kinds of passes:

Push pass : This type of pass is used more than any other passes as it is specially good for fast, accurate passing. However, it is important to note that the push pass is good for short distances only and it may lose its effectiveness if the distance is greater than 5 metres. The ball is comfortably held with both hands. The fingers remain spread out and the elbows drawn in. The fingers remain more or less at the rear half of the ball. The ball is released chest-high with a hard push and at the end of the pass the palms are turned outward. The accuracy and the speed of the pass comes from a quick shape of the fingers, wrist and elbows.

Underhand pass : The ball is held low and is protected by the hips. After a slight backward movement the ball is released with a forward swerving of the arms in the direction of the receiver. The last part of the pass is the wrist action which is executed in continuation of the earlier movements. The ball actually leaves the fingertips and the arms and hands move freely in fine follow-through. Such type of pass is generally used when the ball is received low and a short fast pass is required.

Baseball pass : The ball is first placed in both hands and is brought over and behind the right shoulder. Then stepping forward with the left foot, the ball is transferred to the right hand by taking away the left hand. The ball is released by the action of the shoulder, elbow and wrist and with a fast follow-through by the right arm. A quick flexion of the wrist in the direction of the pass is most essential. The right foot may be taken ahead of the left so as to generate more force. It is extremely useful in clearing the ball from the defending area and in making a fast attack.

Bounce pass : The ball is held the same way as in the push pass but the player holding the ball should be in a comfortable position. The pass is executed with a powerful push so that the ball hits the floor and bounces directly towards the receiver. The bounce should be low in order that the receiver may get the ball above the knees and below the waist. This pass may also be performed with one hand.

Overhead pass : The ball is held with both hands almost directly over the head. The thumbs are under the ball and the fingers are well spread. The pass is made by a quick snap of the wrist and fingers, assisted by slight movements of the shoulders and elbows. This type of pass is excellent for feeding a player stationed within shooting distance of the basket and a player who is moving fast forwards the basket.

Fouls

A foul is an infraction of the rules when personal contact with an opponent or un-sportsmanlike behaviour is involved. It is charged against the offender and consequently penalized according to the provisions of the relevant article of the rules. A personal foul is a player foul which involves contact with an opposing player, whether the ball is alive or dead. Any player shall not block, hold, push, charge, trip, impede the progress of an opponent by extending his arm, shoulder, hip, knee or foot, nor by bending his body into other than a normal position, nor shall he use any rough tactics.

Penalty

A personal foul shall be charged to the offender in all cases. If the foul is committed on a player who is not in the act of shooting, the game shall be resumed by a throw-in by the non-offending team out-of-bounds nearest the place of infraction. If the foul is committed on a player who is in the act of shooting, if the goal is made, it shall count and one free throw shall be awarded. If the foul is committed by a player while his team is in control of the ball, the game shall be resumed by a throw-in by the non-offending team from out-of-bounds nearest the place of infraction.

Skills

In addition to the basics of passing and catching, shooting is a key skill for all players of a team. Because of the pace and pressure of a game, shots at the basket have to be attempted at every opportunity. Apart from when a free throw is used to score, shots at goal may be made from every angle., taken on the move or as the ball rebounds off the basket or backboard after an unsuccessful shot.

A player can aim and throw the ball so that it scores up and over, or jump so that he is able to drop the ball in with a flick of the wrist from above the ring. Further, at the commencement of a player's action there may be an initial stance and in some cases the player may receive the ball on the run and continue his performance.

Tennis

History

Tennis was known by the name of '*Tenez*' in Egypt and some parts of Middle East. The view of the Egyptian town on the Nile was known as *Tinnis* in Arabic. Together with court tennis, the 12th century crusaders brought some of its terms to Europe. The word '*racquet*' or *racket* is derived from the Arab word '*Rahat*'. It means '*Palm of the hand*'. The game was played by wearing gloves on the hands. Court tennis first of all was played by monks.

In 1793, the first references to the game of tennis were published in '*Sporting Magazine*'. This magazine was related to London. In 1873, the references contained therein of a game described as '*Field Tennis*' were very similar to the game of '*Long Tennis*' mentioned in a book '*Games And Sports*'. The first Wimbledon Championship was played in 1877.

India debuted on July 16, 1921 with M. Saleem and S.M. Jacob in the singles and L.S. Deane with A.A. Fyzee in the doubles. They won the tie 4-1 against France in Paris. Deane played the second reverse singles in place of an injured Jacob and won the title. India's Anand Amritraj was the youngest player (16 years) when he played Sri Lanka in the Davis Cup on April 27, 1968.

The court

A tennis court can be of grass, concrete, wood, clay or may be of artificial grass. The court is rectangular with 78 ft. (23.77 m) length and 27 ft. (8.23 m) width for singles. For doubles, it is 78 ft. (23.77 m) long and 36 ft. (10.97 m) wide. The court is divided into two parts with the help of a net across the centre line and then into two service courts and a back court on either side of this by lines on the ground. The court should have sufficient running space around it.

Equipments

Net : The net is suspended from a cord or metal cable attached to the tops of the two posts. The posts are positioned three ft. outside each sideline at the centre of the court. The top of the net must be three ft. above the ground at its centre, at which point the net is also held taut by a vertical white strap.

Racket : The tennis racket looks like a badminton racket but it is heavy and solid than the latter. It is made of wood, aluminium, graphite or such type of material. The maximum length of a racket should be 32 inch and the maximum width should not be more than 12 inch. The head of a racket should be 15 ½ inch in length and 11 ½ inch in width. The head is strung with natural gut or artificial string running horizontally and vertically.

Ball : A tennis ball is usually of yellow or white colour with a fabric cover. The ball is made of rubber. The outer surface should be uniform and in case seams are there, they should be stitchless. The diameter of the ball should be between 2½ to $2_{5/8}$ inch (6.350 – 6.668 cm) and the weight should between 2 to $2_{1/16}$ oz (56.7 to 58.5 g). The ball must rebound to a height of 53-58 inch (134.62 – 147.32 cm) when dropped from a height of 100 inch (254 cm).

Dress : The traditional dress worn by tennis players consists of shirt, shorts of white colour for men and skirt with shirt of white colour for women. Although coloured dress

is also permitted, but it depends on the organizing committee or governing body. The tennis shoes should be fairly lightweight with a reasonable amount of grip.

Game

The winner of the toss decides to accept a choice of ends or the right to serve or receive first. The player taking the first serve stands with his feet behind the base line on the right-hand side of his court. His feet must remain behind the base line and within the imaginary extensions of the centre-mark and the side lines until the ball is played. The ball is then thrown into the air and struck with the racket before it hits the ground. It must land in the receiver's right-hand court to be 'in'. The server has two chances to make a good service, after which the point is lost. Players must win points, games and then sets in order to win a match. The first player to win six games wins a set. A match has a maximum of five sets for men and three for women.

Service

The service shall be delivered in the following manner:
(i)   Immediately before commencing to serve.
(ii)   The server shall stand with both feet at rest behind the base line, and within the imaginary continuations of the centre-mark and side line. The server shall then project the ball by hand into the air in any direction and before it hits the ground strike it with his racket.
(iii)   The delivery shall be deemed to have been completed at the moment of the impact of the racket and ball.
(iv)   A player with the use of only one arm may utilize his racket for the projection.

Foot fault

The server shall throughout the delivery of the service:
(i)   Not change his position by walking or running. The server shall not by slight movements of the feet, which do not materially affect the location originally taken up by him, be deemed "to change his position by walking or running."
(ii)   Not touch, with either foot, any area other than that behind the base-line within the imaginary extension of the centre-mark and side-lines.

Delivery of service

(i)   In delivering the service, the server shall stand alternately behind the right and left halves of the court beginning from the right in every game. If service from a wrong half of the court occurs and is undetected, all play resulting from such wrong service or services shall stand, but the inaccuracy of station shall be corrected immediately it is discovered.

(ii)   The ball served shall pass over the net and hit the ground within the service court which is diagonally opposite, or upon any line bounding such court, before the receiver returns it.

Service fault

The service is a fault:
(i) If the server commits any breach in the rules of service, foot fault or delivery of service.
(ii) If he misses the ball in attempting to strike it.
(iii) If the ball served touches a permanent fixture before it hits the ground.

The Let

In all cases where a 'let' has to be called under the rules, or to provide for an interruption to play, it shall have the following interpretation:
(i) When called solely in respect of a service that one service only shall be replayed.
(ii) When called under any other circumstance, the point shall be replayed.

The service is a 'let' if the ball served touches the net, strap or band, and is otherwise good, or after touching the receiver or anything wears or carries before hitting the ground or if a service or a fault is delivered when the receiver is not ready.

In the case of a 'let', that particular service shall not count, and the server shall serve again, but a service 'let' does not annul a previous fault.

Changing ends

At the end of the first, third and every subsequent alternate game of each set and at the end of each set the players shall change the ends unless the total number of games in such set is even, in which case the change is not made until the end of the first game of the next set. If a mistake is made and the correct sequence is not followed, the players must take up their correct station as soon as the discovery is made and follow their original sequence.

Ball in play

A ball is in the play from the moment at which it is delivered in service. Unless a fault or a 'let' is called it remains in play until the point is decided.

Server wins point

The server wins the point:
(i) If the ball served, not being a let under the rule, touches the receiver or anything he wears or carries, before it hits the ground.
(ii) If the receiver otherwise loses the points as provided by law.

Receiver wins point

The receiver wins point:
(i) If the server serves two consecutive faults.
(ii) If the server otherwise loses the point as provided by rule.

Player loses point

(i) A player loses the point if he fails before the ball in play has hit the ground twice consecutively, to return it directly over the net.
(ii) He volleys the ball and fails to make a good return over when standing outside the court.
(iii) He or his racket or anything which he wears or carries touches the net, posts, singles sticks, cord or metal cable, strap or band or the ground within his opponent's court at any time while the ball is in play.

(iv)   He volleys the ball before it has passed the net.

(v)   He returns the ball in play so that it hits the ground, a permanent fixture, or other object, outside any of the lines which bound his opponent's court.

(vi)   He deliberately and materially changes the shape of his racket during the playing of the point.

(vii) He throws his racket at and hits the ball.

(viii) The ball in play touches him or anything he wears, carries except his racket in his hand or hands.

(ix)   He deliberately carries or catches the ball and touches it with his racket more than once.

Player hinders opponent

If a player commits any act which hinders his opponent in making a stroke, then it is deliberate, he shall lose the point or if involuntary, the point shall be replayed.

Ball falls on line

During serving or receiving the ball sometimes falls on line. This is regarded as falling in the court bounded by that line.

Ball touches permanent fixtures

In play if the ball touches a permanent fixture except net, posts, singles sticks, cord or metal cable, strap or band after it has hit the ground, the player who struck it wins the points, if before it hits the ground, his opponent wins the point.

Good return

The following are the good returns:

(i)   If the ball, served or returned, hits the ground within the proper court and rebounds or is blown back over the net, and the player whose turn it is to strike reaches over the net and plays the ball.

(ii) If a player succeeds in returning the ball, served or in play, which strikes a ball lying on the court.

(iii) If the ball touches the net, posts, singles sticks, cord or metal cable, strap or band. Provided that it passes over any of them and hits the ground within the court.

(iv) If a player's racket passes over the net after he has returned the ball, provided the ball passes the net before being played and properly returned.

(v) If the ball is returned outside the posts or singles sticks, either above or below the level of the top of the net, even though it touches the post or singles sticks, provided that it hits the ground within the proper court.

Hindrance of player

If a player is hindered in making a stroke by anything not within his control, except a permanent fixture of the court, or except as provided for in law, a let shall be called.

Scoring

Game : If a player wins his first point, the score is called 15 for that player; on winning his second point, the score is called 30; on winning the third point, the score is 40 and on winning fourth point by a player is scored 'Game' for that player. If both players have won the 3 points, the score is called 'Deuce' and the next point won by any player is scored as advantage for that player. If the same player wins the next point, he wins the game; however if the other player wins the next point the score is again called deuce, and so on, until a player wins the 2 points immediately following the score at deuce, wins the game.

Set : A player who first wins 6 games, with a clear margin of 2 games over his opponent, wins a set. If required, a set can be extended to achieve the margin of 2 games. As an alternative to this system, the 'Tie-Breaker' system of scoring can be adopted, provided it is announced before the commencement of the match. The tie-break shall operate when the score reaches 6 games-all in any set, except the third and fifth set of three-set or five-set match respectively.

The system used in tie-break game is as under:

Singles : A player who wins first 7 points, provided he leads by 2 points, wins the game and the set. If the score is 6-all, the game shall be extended till a margin of 2 points is achieved. Numerical scoring shall be used throughout the tie-break game. The receiver shall be the server for the second and third point, thereafter each player shall serve for 2 consecutive points until the winner is decided. The first service is started from the right court and thereafter alternatively from the left and the right courts. In case a wrong service is detected during the game, it should be corrected immediately, but all previous play shall stand. Players should change their ends after 6 points and at the end of the tie-break game.

Doubles: In doubles the procedure for single shall apply. The player whose turn it is to serve shall be the server for the first point. Thereafter each player shall serve in rotation for two points, in the same order as previously in that set, until the winners of the game and set have been decided.

Maximum number of sets

In the match of tennis, a maximum number of sets shall be 5 or where women take part 3.

Court officials

If in any match a referee is not appointed, umpire will make all the decisions. But where a referee is appointed, an appeal can be made to him on question of law, and in such case the decision of the referee shall be final. In matches where linesmen, net-cord judges, foot-fault judges are appointed, they made the final decisions on questions of fact except that if in the opinion of an umpire a clear mistake has been made, he shall have the right to change the decision of an assistant. He may postpone a match on account of darkness, or the condition of the ground, or weather. In case of postponement the score and courts shall hold good, unless the referee and the players unanimously agree otherwise.

Breaks

The game starts and continues from the first service of the play until it concludes in accordance with the following provisions:

(i)   It should be not suspended, delayed or interfered to enable a player to recover his strength, breath or physical conditions. However, in case of an injury to the player, the game may be suspended for 3-5 minutes.

(ii)   In case of service fault, the second service should be made without any delay. The receiver must be ready to receive when the server is ready.

(iii)　The umpire may suspend or delay game at any time if he considers it appropriate. In case when clothing footwear or any equipment is required the umpire may suspend the game, until the necessary adjustments are fulfilled.

(iv)　Generally the warm-up time should not exceed 5 minutes and it should be announced before the commencement of the match.

(v)　On any type of violation of these principles by any player the umpire may give a warning or disqualify the offenders.

Coaching

A player (s) may receive coaching during the playing of a game in a team competition. A player (s) may receive the coaching from captain who is sitting on the court only when he changes ends at the end of a game, but not when he changes ends during a tie-break game.

A player may not receive coaching during the playing of any other match. The provisions of this rule must be strictly constructed. After due warning an offending player may be disqualified. When an approved point penalty system is in the game, the umpire shall impose penalties according to that system.

Change of ball

In some games the balls are to be changed after 9 specified number of games. If the balls were not changed in correct sequence, the mistake shall be corrected when the player or pair, who should have served with new balls, is next due to serve. Thereafter the balls shall be changed so that the number of games between changes shall be that originally agreed.

Doubles game

Service order

The service order in doubles game is little different than singles game. The pair who have to serve in the first game of each set shall decide which partner shall do so and the opposing pair shall decide similarly for the second game. The partner of the player who served in the first game shall serve in the third, the partner of the player who served in the second game shall serve in the fourth, and so on in the same order in all the subsequent games.

Receiving order

The pair who have to receive the service in the first game shall decide which partner shall receive the first service and that partner shall continue to receive the first service in every odd game throughout the set. The opposing pair shall likewise decide which partner shall continue to receive the first service in every even game throughout that set. Both the partners shall receive the service alternately throughout each game.

Out of turn

If any partner serves out of his turn the partner who ought to have served shall serve as soon as the mistake is discovered, but all points scored, and any faults served before such discovery, shall be reckoned. If a game shall have been completed before such discovery, the order of service remains as altered.

Receiving errors

During a game, if the order of receiving the service is changed by the receivers, it shall remain as altered until the end of the game in which the mistake is discovered, but the partners shall resume their original order of receiving in the next game of that set in which they are receivers of the service.

Playing the ball

The ball shall be alternately played by one or the other player of the opposing pairs, and if a player touches the ball in play with his racket in contravention of this rule, his opponent wins the point.

Skills

Tennis requires the same mobility, ball control and strategic thinking as most racket sports. All the players also need to be able to combine powerful, robust shots with a high degree of accuracy. The service is an essential stroke to get right. Because the server has complete control of the ball this is an opportunity to score points and quickly gain the upper hand. The forehand and backhand drives are basic ground-strokes. They are strong shots, usually played from near the base-line and travelling the length of the court. An overhead smash is another potential point-scoring stroke. The action is similar to that used for the service.

Badminton

History

Its history indicates that this game was played first of all in England. Two games were played by the people of England, named 'Poona' and 'Battledore'. The word 'Poona' means 'Shuttlecock'. Thus Badminton is a combination of two games. Its name has been derived from the county residence 'Badminton' of the Duke of Beaufort. Initially it gained popularity amongst the British army officers who took it to India. As some of the officers were friends of the Duke of Beaufort, thus they were invited to play this game. The officers then took the sport to India where they played it first time in Karachi.

The first laws of badminton were drawn up at Poona (India) in 1870 and they underwent gradually changes with time. Its first rules were printed in Karachi in 1877. British army personnel were largely responsible for the adaptation of the sport and formation of the earliest English clubs in seaside resorts.

In 1893, the Badminton Association of England was founded. From England touring players and teams pioneered enthusiasm for it to Denmark and USA. The International Badminton Federation was founded in 1934 and the nations from all over world joined it. After that it became an international game.

In India, the game has been very popular after the First Asian Games. The first tournament was held by the Punjab State Championship in 1929. The Badminton Association of India was formed in 1934.

Badminton hall

Badminton court is constructed in an indoor hall. Whenever possible, natural light should be allowed to come through the windows of the badminton hall. In case, if there is no sufficient natural light, there should be arrangements for electric lights in the hall. Any system moving in the air should not be installed in the hall. The root of the hall should not be less than 9m high from the court.

The court

The badminton court should be rectangular in size and laid out to the measurements as per law, defined by the lines ½" wide. All the lines should be easily distinguishable and preferably be coloured white or dark yellow. The length of a court which can be used for singles as well as doubles shall be 13.40 m (44 ft.) and width 6.10 m (20 ft.). The surface of the floor should be made with wood or synthetic. The court shall be divided in two equal parts. A centre line should be marked in the centre of the court, with the help of two posts. The centre line between the right and left service court shall be equally divided. All the lines generally mark out a court which can be used for both singles and doubles, although a singles-only court is possible.

Equipments

Posts : Two post shall be fixed with the centre line of the court. They shall be 159 cm (5 ft 1 inch) in height from the floor and shall be sufficiently firm to keep the net tight as provided in law and shall be placed on the side boundary lines of the court. The posts should be made of iron or any suitable metal.

Net : The net shall be made of good cord and of dark colour. The thickness of the cord should not be less than 15 mm. The net shall be firmly stretched from one post to the other. It should be 76 cm in depth. The top of the net should be 152 cm in height from the floor and 155 cm at the posts. It should be edged with a double tape of 75 mm in white colour and supported by a cord or cable run through the tape and stretched over and flush with the top of the posts.

Shuttle : A shuttle can be the original feathered or the newer synthetic model. Both must have a rounded base of 25-8 mm diameter and a total weight of between 4.74 g to 5.50 g (appx 0.2 oz). The speed of the shuttle depends on the weight, temperature and barometric pressure. Occasionally it is worth checking that the shuttle is in playing condition.

To do this, hold the shuttle over the base line and use an underarm stroke to hit it at an upward angle, straight to the other back boundary line. If the speed is correct it will land not less than 530 mm and not more than 990 mm short of the opposite line.

Racket : A racket is made of steel/aluminium /ceramic or graphite having an ideal length of 680 mm (27 inch) and 230 mm (9 inch) in overall width. The racket has three parts – frame, shaft and grip. The stringed area must be flat and of a uniform pattern. Natural gut gives the best performance for the strings.

Dress : For a man, shorts and a lightweight shirt are practical, while a woman may replace the shorts with a skirt. The clothing must allow ease of movement.

Game

The game of badminton may be divided into two categories – singles and doubles. Two players compete for the opportunity to serve and then, hopefully, score points. If the player serving wins a rally they also win a point. If the server loses a rally, the service passes to the opponent. If the player loses another fault while his opponent is the server, a point goes to the opponent. As above, except the serve is passed on from one player to his partner before it can be 'lost' to the receiving side.

Officials

There shall be one umpire, one referee, one service judge, and line judges or linemen will be appointed. The umpire will be the overall incharge of the match. He shall report to the referee, who will be overall incharge of the tournament. Service judge will call the service faults and line judge shall indicate whether the shuttle is 'in' or 'out'. If three linesmen are available, two should take a back boundary line and long service line each, the third the sideline farthest from the umpire.

Starting

Before the commencement of the game, there shall be a 'toss'. Toss decides who will serve first from which end of the court and the game will start. The first serve is an underarm shot from the right service court to the receiver in the court diagonally opposite. Points may only be scored when serving. Generally a match consists of three games, each won by the first side to reach 15 points. Women's singles are won by the first to win 11 points.

Scoring

The opposing sides shall play the best of three games unless otherwise arranged. Only the serving side can add a point to its score. In doubles and men's singles a game is won by the first side to score 15 points, except as provided in the law. In ladies singles a game is won by the first side to score 11 points. If the score becomes 13-all or 14-all, the side which first scored 13 or 14 shall have the choice of 'setting' or 'not setting' the game. This choice can be made when the score is first reached and must be made before the next service is delivered. The relevant side is given the opportunity to set at 14-all despite any previous decision not to set by that side or the opposing side at 13-all. If the game has been set, the score is called 'Love-all' and the side first scoring the set number of points wins the game. The side winning a game serves first in the next game.

Change of ends

Players shall change ends:
(i)   At the end of the first game.
(ii) Prior to the beginning of the third game.
(iii) In the third game, or in a one-game match, when the leading score reaches 6 in a game of 11 points or 8 in a game of 15 points.
(iv) When players omit to change ends as indicated by law, they shall do so immediately the mistake is discovered and the existing score shall stand.

Service

The service should be done immediately. The server and the receiver shall stand diagonally opposite service courts without touching the boundary lines of the service court. The server's racket shall initially hit the base of the shuttle while the whole of the shuttle is below the server's waist. The movement of the server's racket must continue forwards after the start of the service until the service is delivered and the flight of the shuttle shall be upward from the server's racket to pass over the net so that, if not intercepted, if falls in the receiver's service court. The service is delivered when, once started the shuttle hit by the server's racket or the shuttle lands on the floor. In doubles, the partners may take up any positions which do not upset the opposing server or receiver.

Service – court errors

A service court error has been made when a player:
(i) Has served out of turn.
(ii) Has served from the wrong service court.
(iii) Standing in the wrong service court, was prepared to receive the service and it has been delivered.

If there is a 'Let' because of a service-court error, the rally is replayed and the error corrected. If a service-court error is not to be corrected, play in that game shall proceed without changing the player's new service courts.

Faults

(i)   If a service is not corrected.
(ii)   If the server, in attempting to serve, misses the shuttle.
(iii) If, on service, the shuttle is caught on the net and remains suspended on top or, on service after passing over the net, is caught in the net.
(iv)   If in play, the shuttle lands outside the boundaries of the court, passes through or under the net, fails to pass the net, touches the roof, ceiling or side walls, touches the person or dress of a player or touches any other object or person outside the immediate surroundings of the court.
(v)   When the initial point of contact with the shuttle is not on the striker's side of the net.
(vi)   When the shuttle is in play, a player touches the net or its supports with racket, person or dress, invades an opponent's court with racket or obstructs an opponent.
(vii) A player deliberately distracts an opponent by any action such as shouting or making guestures.

(viii) Be caught and held of the racket and then slung during the execution of a stroke, touches a player's racket and continues towards the back of that player's court.

(ix) If a player is guilty of flagrant, repeated of persistent offences under the law.

Let

"Let" is called by the umpire or by a player to halt play. A 'Let' may be given for any unforeseen or accidental occurrence. If a shuttle is caught on the net and remains suspended on top, or after passing over the net is caught in the net, it is a 'Let' except during service. If during service, the receiver and the server are both faulted at the same time, it shall be a 'Let' and when a line judge is unsighted and the umpire is unable to make any decision. When a 'Let' occurs, the play since the last service shall not count and the player who served shall serve again.

Shuttle not in play

A shuttle is not in play when it:
(i) Strikes the net and remains attached there or suspended on top.
(ii) Strikes the net or post and starts to fall towards the surface of the court on the striker's side of the net.
(iii) Hits the surface of the court.
(iv) A 'Fault' or 'Let' has occurred.

Continuous play, misconduct, penalties

(i) Game shall be continuous from the first service until the match is concluded, except as allowed in the laws.

(ii) An interval shall be given of five minutes between the second and third games.

(iii) When necessitated by circumstances not within the control of the players, the umpire may suspend play for such a period as the umpire may consider necessary, if play be suspended the existing score shall stand and play be resumed from that point.

(iv) Under no circumstances shall play be suspended

to enable a player to recover his strength or wind, or to receive instruction or advice.

(v) Except in the intervals provided for the game, no player shall be permitted to receive advice during a match.

(vi) The umpire shall be sole judge of any suspension of play.

(vii) A player shall not deliberately cause suspension of play, deliberately interfere with the speed of the shuttle and behave in an offensive manner.

(viii) The umpire shall administer any breach of laws.

(ix) Where a referee has not been appointed, the responsible official shall have the power to disqualify.

Skills

A successful player needs to be extremely fit and alert in order to keep up with the quick fire rallies that characterize badminton. Although control of the racket with the arm and wrist is all important, balance, speed and clever footwork are also vital if a player is to use stroke skills anywhere inside the court at a moment's notice.

Baseball

History

Baseball is an American game. Though authentic records are not available as to the date of origin, it is however an accepted fact that baseball had its birth early in the 20th century. This is the national summer sport of the U.S., although its popularity is now firmly established in countries as far afield as Japan, Netherlands and Australia. The roots are generally traced back to the 1700s, when similar game of rounders was introduced by English settlers to the American colonies.

The history of the game is closely connected with that of indoor baseball which is a modified form of the regular outdoor game. The credit goes to George W. Hancock who exploited an interesting situation and raised it to the status of a recognized game. The game was first played at Farragut Boat Club, Chicago and became a regular weekly sport. This game can be rightly considered as the forerunner of modern baseball.

The rules were drawn up by Mr Hancock himself, to suit the needs of his modification. As an attempt to further popularise the game, the National Playground Ball Association of U.S. was founded in 1908. Later on in 1923, the Amateur Softball Association of America came into existence. Further in 1927 the American Physical Education Association formed a set of rules specially for women.

The game travelled to the shores of India and became popular here. The game is extremely well suited to local climate and other conditions in India and because of the small playing area required, it creates no major problems and satisfies the recreational needs of youngsters of schools and colleges.

The field

The playing area of the baseball is known as diamond. The diamond should be covered with grass or artificial turf. It should consist of an outfield – a 90 ft square with 90 ft being the distance between each base. Home base is marked by a five-sided slab of whitened rubber. First, second and third bases are marked by 15-inch square white canvas bags, attached to the ground. The pitcher's plate is a rectangular slab of whitened rubber. It consists the size of 24-inch long and 6-inch wide. The distance between the pitcher's plate and home base is 60 ft 6 inch.

Equipments

Bat : The bat is a smooth round stick. It should be made of one piece of hardwood or formed from a block of wood consisting of two or more pieces of wood bonded together with adhesive in such a way that the grain directions of all pieces is essentially parallel to the length of bat. It may also be made with bamboo, plastic, graphite or magnesium. But it should have a clear finish. The length of the bat should not be more than 42 inches and shall not exceed 38 ounces in weight. The diameter at thickest part must not be more than 7 cm. A safety knob of ¼ inch producing a 90° angle from the handle must be included on plastic, bamboo or wood bats. It can be moulded, welded or mechanically fastened.

Ball : The ball is spherical. The centre of the ball may be made of No. 1 quality, long fibre *kapok* or mixture of cork and rubber, hand or machine wound, with a fine quality twisted yarn and covered with latex or rubber cement. The cover of the ball may also be made of synthetic material. The ball must consist a weight of 5 – 5¼ oz and the circumference of 9 – 9¼ inch.

Dress

The league matches may require a team to wear one distinctive colour of uniform or they may allow two sets – a white one for home games and a different colour for away games. Uniforms must not feature glass buttons, polished metal or any patterns that might suggest the shape of a baseball. The catcher may wear a leather mitt which should not be more than 38 inch in circumference and 15½ inch in length. The first batsman wear a leather glove or mitt which should not be more than 12 inch in length. All other fielders may wear a leather glove. The pitcher's glove must not be white or grey. The catcher wears a protective helmet and the players, during bat, must also wear helmet.

Game

The match is played between two teams. Each team consists of nine players. The fielding team players takes the following positions on the field:
— Pitcher
— Catcher
— First Baseman
— Second Baseman
— Third Baseman
— Shortstop
— Left Fielder
— Centre Fielder
— Right Fielder

The batting team prepares themselves to bat. The object of the game is to strike the ball and then complete the circuit to first, second and third and back to home base touching each on the way to score a run. The team which scores the most runs wins. One run is scored when each time a runner completes the circuit of bases. If the ball is hit far enough this may be completed in one go for a home run. A home run is also scored if a fly ball passes over the fence or into the stands, at least 250 ft away from home base. A game consists of nine innings, unless it is extended to resolve a tied score.

The batter

The batter shall take his position in the batter's box promptly when it is time to bat. If he refuses to take his position in batter's box during his time of bat, the umpire shall order the pitcher to pitch and shall call 'strike' on each such pitch. The batter may take his proper position after any such pitch and the regular ball and strike count shall continue, but if he does not take his position before three strikes are called, he shall be declared out. His legal position shall be with both feet within the batter's box. A batter may be out in the following ways:

(i)   He attempts to hit a third strike and the ball touches him.
(ii)   He bounds foul on third strike.
(iii) His first base is tagged before he touches first base after hitting a foul ball.
(iv)   His fair or foul ball is legally caught by a player.
(v)   An infield fly is declared.
(vi)   With two out, a runner on third base, and two strikes on the batter, the runner attempts to steal home base or a legal pitch and the ball touches the runner in batter's strike zone, the batter becomes out.
(vii) A fair ball touches him before touching any fielder.

The runner

A runner aquires the right to an unoccupied base when he touches it before he is out. He is entitled to it until he is put out or forced to vacate it for another runner. Each runner, other than batter may without liability to be put out, advance one base when there is a ball or a fielder after catching a fly ball falls into a bench or stand. Each runner including the batter-runner may, without liability to be put out advance to home base, scoring a run, if a fair ball goes out of the playing field in flight and he touched all bases legally or two bases, if a fair ball bounces or is deflected into the stands outside the first or third base foul lines. A runner may be out in the following ways:

(i)   He is tagged, when the ball is alive, while off his base.
(ii)   He attempts to score on a play in which the play at home base before two are out.
(iii) He intentionally interferes with a thrown ball.
(iv)   He fails to retouch his base after a fair or foul ball is legally caught before he or his base is tagged by any fielder.
(v)   He runs more than 3 ft away from a direct line between bases to avoid being tagged unless his action is to avoid interference with a fielder fielding a batted ball.
(vi)   He passes a preceding runner before such runner is out.

(vii)   He fails to return at once to first base after overrunning or oversliding that base.

The pitcher

The pitcher shall stand facing the batter. His entire pivot foot on, or in front of and touching and not off the end of the pitcher's plate, and the other foot free. From this position any natural movement associated with his delivery of the ball to the batter commits him to the pitch without interruption. Set position shall be indicated by the pitcher when he stands facing the batter with his entire pivot foot on or in front of the pitcher's plate. If he makes any illegal pitch with the bases unoccupied, it shall be called a ball unless the batter reaches first base on a hit, an error, a base on balls, a hit batter or otherwise the pitches shall not bring his pitching hand in contact with his month or lips while he is in 18 ft. circle.

When the bases are unoccupied, the pitcher shall deliver the ball to the batter with 20 seconds after he receives the ball. Each time the pitcher delays the game by violating this rule, the umpire shall call 'Ball'. The intent of this rule is to avoid unnecessary delays.

Umpire

In world championships and series, there are six umpires appointed: One each at home plate and three at bases and one near the extremity of each of the two foul lines. When only one umpire is used, he usually stands behind the pitcher in order to call balls and strikes and at the same time to be as close as possible to the bases.

Terms

Throwback : For fielders in the outfield of a good return throw is vital. The fielder must be able to make a strong accurate throw ahead of the runners to stop them moving on.

Run out : Most players are actually dismissed by being run out. Typically when a fielder throws the ball to a baseman so quickly that a runner forced to run is beaten.

Tagged out : Occasionally runners are put out when a fielder 'tags' him with the ball when he is running between bases.

Balk : A balk occurs when there is a runner on a base and the pitcher commits an illegal act. This may be one of many things, such as feinting.

Big swing : A baseball is difficult to hit well so scoring is low. The key for the batter is keeping a low, even swing.

Skills:

A good eye and a powerful swing are the basic skills of the batter. He must be able to make a snap decision to leave any pitch that looks like it may be a 'ball', since he has so few chances to strike the ball. He may tap the ball carefully to place it somewhere within the infield. To match the speed or runners progressing from base to base, fielders must be expert at retrieving and passing the ball, while the baseman cannot afford to fumble a catch when the difference between them catching the ball and a runner sliding into base may be a split second. The pitcher also requires an enormous amount of intelligence, concentration and excellent skills.

Table Tennis

History

Historically, the game of table tennis is very old. It was developed as an ordinary indoor game named 'Ping-Pong' – probably an onomatopoeic expression derived out of the sound the ball makes on its impact upon the table – towards the end of the last decade of the 19th century. It is believed that the game was a product of the efforts made in the 19th century to promote it. E.C. Goode of Pufney used the first time wooden racket with plumped rubber covering on the blade.

The game lost its appeal around 1904 and did not revive until after World War - I when in 1921, the Ping-Pong Association was established in Britain. The name of the Association was changed to Table Tennis Association in 1926. After that this became a worldwide governing body, looking to the game's growing popularity, a national representative conference was arranged in London during 1926-27. It approved the new constitution of the game, devised to make the game more interesting and mature. In 1933 the U.S. Table Tennis Association was formed as one of its affiliates.

The first European Table Tennis Competition was arranged in 1966 in Wembley. 33 nations participated in this competition. Thus the game continued to grow in popularity all over the world. Japan, China, Hungary, Indonesia and Czechoslovakia have made especially strong showing in international play.

India arranged the First National Championship in 1938. It was organized in Calcutta where M. Ayub won the title in the final. Yet its reputation as a fun pastime for all ages and abilities belies the fact that at competition level players have amazing skills.

Playing arena

There is no specific mention about the size of the table tennis hall in any of the law. But it should be bigger and better as it would provide more room for the movements of the players and high rising shots. Normally on both sides of the table, there should be a space of 5 ft. and 8 ft. on the front and the back side of the table. The overall size of the arena should be about 15 x 25 sq. ft.

The floor of the arena should be resilient, splinter-proof, stable, non-skid and hard wearing. The colour of the floor should be dark because in the light coloured background the visibility of the ball decreases. The walls surrounding the playing arena should not be of dazzling white colour, especially the height of the walls which meets the normal eye-level. A dark dull-colour-painted wall is ideal for this purpose. The arena should have the sufficient lighting and ventilating facilities.

Equipments

The table : A rectangular table is used to play the game. The length of the table must 2.74 m (9 ft) and the width must be 1.52 m (5 ft). The height of the table from the floor shall be 76 cm. The playing surface shall be made of any material and shall yield a uniform bounce of abut 23 cm when a standard ball is dropped on to it from a height of 30 cm. The playing surface shall be uniformly dark coloured (green, blue and malt) with white marking lines. The playing surface shall be divided into two equal courts by a vertical line not running parallel with the end lines and shall be continuous over the whole area of each court. For doubles, each court shall be divided into two equal half courts by a white centre line (3 mm wide) running parallel with the side lines. If the dirt gets accumulated on the top of the surface, gently rub it off without exerting any force in doing so. The players do not wipe their sweat with the edge of the table and nobody should sit over the table.

The net : A net shall be suspended from a cord attached to two posts, each 6 inch high and joined to the table with clamps. The length of the net shall be 1.83 m with a height of 15.25 cm above the top of the table. Having tied the upper cord, the lower cord should be tied properly. The amount of tension should be somewhat less in it than you have stressed the upper cord with.

The bat or racket : The racket is the main weapon of the player. One should select the racket with utmost care. It may be of any size, shape or weight, but must have a flat blade of even thickness. The blade must consist of 85% natural wood and should be covered with pimpled or sandwich rubber on the top of the striking sides. The pimples may face inwards or outwards. The handle of the bat can be covered with any material which gives a good grip. For international competitions one side of the racket shall be red and the other side should be blue. The racket should be kept in a proper cover and away from moisture and sunshine. Specially the sandwich rackets lose their effectiveness soon if exposed to the rigours of the season.

The ball : The ball for table tennis shall be spherical and made of celluloid or a similar plastic. The colour of the ball may be white, yellow or orange. The diameter of the ball shall be 38 mm and the weight shall be 2.5 gms. It is always better to use a ball which bears a stamp of the National Table Tennis Association.

Dress : The clothing for table tennis players shall be a short-sleeved shirt and shorts for men and a skirt in place of shorts for women. The main colour must be clearly different to that of the ball, and the shirts of opposing players must be different from each other. Their shoes shall be of flat sole for getting a good grip on the floor of the arena.

Game

Table tennis is played by either two players which is called 'singles' or by two teams consisting two players in each team which is called 'doubles'. In singles, the players take it in turns to strike the ball after it has bounced once at their court so that it passes over the net and into their opponent's court. Points are scored by winning rallies. In doubles, there is a set striking order to follow. The service is received by one opponent. The ball must then be struck by the server's partner and then, finally, by the receiver's partner. This sequence is maintained throughout a rally.

Officials

In world, continental and open international championship one umpire and one assistant umpire shall be appointed for each individual match. In other competitions an assistant umpire may be appointed at the discretion of the referee.

The umpire shall sit or stand at the side of the table in line with the net. He shall be solely responsible for the following:

(i) He will check all the playing equipments and the playing conditions.

(ii) He shall control the order of servicing and receiving and ends and correcting any errors.

(iii) Calling the scores, in accordance with the procedure set out under the head scoring.

(iv) Ensuring observation of the regulations concerning advice to the players and the behaviour of the players.

The assistant umpire shall sit opposite, in line with the net and shall be responsible for timing, duration of game, counting the strokes, deciding whether the ball in play touches the side of table facing him, the top edge of the playing surface on that side or neither.

Service

(i) At the start of the service the ball shall be stationary resting freely on the flat palm of the server's free hand, behind the end line and above the level of the playing surface.

(ii) The server shall then project the ball near vertically upwards, without imparting spin, so that it rises at least 6 inch after leaving the palm of the free hand and then falls without touching anything before being struck.

(iii) As the ball is falling, the server shall strike it so that it touches first his court and then, after passing over or around the net assembly, touches directly the receiver's court.

(iv) The ball and the racket shall be above the level of the playing surface from the last moment at which the ball is stationary before being projected until it is struck.

(v)   When the ball is struck it shall be behind the server's end line but not farther back than the part of the server's body, other than his arm, head or leg, which is farthest from his end line.

(vi) It is the responsibility of the player to serve so that the umpire or assistant umpire can see that he complies with the requirements for a good service.

(vii) Exceptionally, the umpire may relax the requirements for a good service where he is notified, before play begins, that compliance is prevented by physical disability.

Return

A ball having been served or returned in play shall be struck so that it passes directly over or around the net and directly touches the opponent's court, provided that, if the ball, having been served or returned in play, returns with its own imetus over or around the net, it may be struck, while still in play, so that it directly touches the opponent's court.

The let

The rally shall be a let:

(i)   While serving, the ball in passing over or around the net assembly, touches it, provided the service is otherwise good or the ball is obstructed by the receiver or his partner.

(ii) If the service is delivered when the receiving player or pair is not ready.

(iii) If failure to make a good service or a good return.

(iv) If play is interrupted by the umpire or the assistant umpire.

(v)   If in doubles, the wrong player serves or receives the ball.

Point

A player shall score a point, unless the rally is a let:

(i)   If his opponent fails to make a good service or a good return.

(ii) If the ball after his opponent has struck it, passes over his end line without having touched his court.

(iii)   If he volleys or obstructs the ball except as provided in the Law.

(iv)   If his opponent, or anything his opponent wears or carries, moves the playing surface.

(v)   If his opponent's free hand touches the playing surface or his wearing clothes or anything he carries touches the net.

(vi)   If the ball, after he has made a good service or a good return, touches anything other than the net assembly before being struck by his opponent.

(vii)   In doubles game, if the opponent strikes the ball out of proper sequence.

(viii)   If under the expedite system, he makes, or he and his partner make 13 successive good returns including the return of the service.

Serving, receiving or ends – out of order

If a player serves or receives out of turn, the play shall be interrupted by the umpire as soon as the error is discovered and shall resume with those players serving and receiving who should be server and receiver respectively at the score that has been reached, according to the sequence established at the beginning of the match and, in doubles, to the order of serving chosen by the pair having the right to serve first in the game during which the error discovered.

If the players have not changed ends when they should have done so, play shall be interrupted by the umpire as soon as the error is discovered and shall resume with the players at the ends at which they should be at the score that has been reached, according to the sequence established at the beginning of the game. All points shall be reckoned after the discovery of the error.

Expedite system

The expedite system shall come into operation if a game is unfinished after 15 minutes play, unless both players or pairs have scored at least 19 points or at any earlier time at the request of players or pairs.

If the ball is in play when the time limit is reached, play shall be interrupted by the umpire and shall resume with service by the player who served the rally that was interrupted. If the ball is not in play when the time limit is reached, play shall resume with service by the player who received in the immediately preceding rally of the game.

Thereafter, each player shall serve for one point in turn until the end of the game and if the receiving player or pair makes 13 good returns the receiver shall score a point.

Once introduced, this system shall remain in operation until the game's end.

Skills

Good anticipation and reaction skills, stamina and coordination will improve any player's game. There are two types of grips which are used. The first is similar to the 'shaking hands grip' used in many other racket games. The second is 'penholder grip' – the handle is held close to the base of the blade, as if it were a pen. Although this grip allows a much faster recovery time since only one side of the bat is ever used, it can make it difficult to return tricky backhand or angle shots.

Players will often try to confuse opponents by turning the bat in their hands while waiting for the return – 'twiddling'. If the bat has two different surface materials the ball will rebound differently according to which one is used. The opponent will therefore not know what sort of return to expect until the last minute.

Handball

History

Handball is one of the oldest games of all—probably played in ancient Greece. It is played throughout the world. The game of handball was introduced by a German gymnast. His name was Konar Kota. He framed some of its rules and regulations and the game was recognised as an athletic event. In 1928 Olympics of Amstendam, handball was a demonstrated game. In 1932, this was introduced as a regular game. This version is the fast-moving team game.

The court

The playing area is called court. It is divided in two halves by a centre line parallel to the goal-lines and two goal-areas. It is rectangular in shape with 40 m length and 20 m width.

Equipments

Goalpost : Each goalpost shall be placed on the centre of each goal-line. A goal consists of 2 m upright post equidistant from the corners of the playing area placed 3 m apart and 2 m high firmly fixed to the ground and firmly joined by a horizontal crossbar. The posts and the crossbar shall be made of wood or light metal and shall be square of 8 × 8 cm.

The ball : The ball must be spherical and consist of a rubber bladder inside it. The outer case must not be too shiny or slippery. The weight of the ball must be between 425 gm to 475 gm for men and youths. The ball for women and juniors shall weigh 325 gm to 400 gm. The circumference of the ball for men should be 58 to 60 cm and for women 54-56 cm. Two balls must be available at the start of the game, although the one chosen is then used solely throughout. It must not be changed during the game except in unavoidable circumstances.

Dress

All the players of a team must wear the same colour of dress. Wearing of sport shoes and their colours must be clearly distinguishable from the other team. Generally shirt with shorts for men and shirt with skirt for women is prescribed for the game. The goalkeepers of both teams should wear colours that distinguish them from all the other players and each other. Armlet around the upper arm is necessary to wear for both captains.

Team

Each team must have 12 players with a maximum of 7 players on the court including the goalkeeper and 5 players as substitute. Each team is having a captain who leads the whole team.

Game

The game starts with toss between both captains. Team winning the toss has the the option of choice of ends or beginning the game with a throw-off. The player taking it does so from the centre of the court. All the other players must be in their own half of the court and the players of non-starting team must be at least 3 m from the player taking the throw. Teams score goals by getting the ball into their opponent's goal. A goal in scored when the ball completely crosses the goal line and passes into a goal. The team with maximum number of goals wins the match.

Free throw

A free throw shall be awarded:
(i) For wasting the time and passive play.
(ii) Any infringements by the goalkeeper.
(iii) Interruption of play without an infringement.
(iv) For entering or leaving the playing ground in a faulty manner.
(v) For infringement by court player in the goal-area.
(vi) For ungentlemanly conduct.

The free throw may be taken immediately without any of the referee blowing his whistle. When the player taking the free throw has taken the correct position, he shall not be allowed either to put the ball on the ground and pick it up again or to bounce it. A free throw must not be awarded if a player remains in full control of the ball in spite of the infringement.

Goal throw

A goal throw is awarded when the ball crosses the outer goal line, having last been touched by a member of the team attacking the goal or by the goalkeeper in the act of defending the goal. The goal throw is executed by means of the goalkeeper throwing the ball into the playing area, from a position inside the goal area. The goalkeeper is not allowed to touch the ball again until it has been touched by another player.

Penalty throw

A penalty throw is taken as a shot goal within 3 seconds from the referee's signal. Once the penalty throw has been taken, the ball may not be played by any court player until it has touched the goalkeeper or the goal. Whilst the penalty throw if being taken all players of the defending team must stand at least 3 m from the thrower. The player taking the penalty throw must not touch or cross 7 m line before the ball has left his hands. The reasons for awarding the penalty throw are:

(i) If there is an unwarranted whistle signal which destroys a clear goal-scoring opportunity.

(ii) When a goalkeeper enters the goal area in possession of the ball.

(iii) When a court player enters his own goal area to gain an advantage over an attacking opponent who is in possession of the ball.

(iv) When a clear goal-scoring opportunity is destroyed by interference of someone who is not authorized to be on the court.

Throw-in

A throw-in is awarded against the team to last touch the ball if it completely crosses the sideline, on the ground or in the air. The throw-in is taken from the place from where the ball crossed the side line. A throw-in may also be awarded if a defender deflects the ball over the outer goal line in which case it is taken from intersection of this line and the side line. The opponents must stay at least 3 m from the player taking the throw-in.

Punishments

A warning can be given for infringements concerning the approach to an opponent and which are to be punished progressively; unsporting conduct by any player; infringement of the rules when an opponent is attempting to execute a throw.

A suspension of 2 minutes shall be given for an incorrect substitution or for entering the court contrary to the rules, if a player fails to place the ball down on to the floor, immediately, when a decision for an infringement has been made against an attacking team, in consequence of a disqualification of a player or team official, for repeated unsporting conduct by a player on the court etc. the decision to suspend a player must be clearly indicated to the player concerned by the referee raising one arm in the air with two fingers extended.

Disqualification

If any player who is not entitled to participate enters the court; for serious infringements relating to the approach to an opponent; for repeated unsporting conduct by a team official or a player·outside the court; for serious unsporting conduct by anybody; for an assault by a team official.

During awarding of disqualification the referee shall indicate the punishment by the holding up of a red card. The player or the official must leave the court and substitution area immediately.

Referee's throw

When the ball has touched the roof or fixed equipment above the playing court, an interruption of the game is caused through to infringement of the rules and while neither side was in possession of the ball and the rules have been infringed simultaneously, on the court, by the players of both teams, the game shall be restarted by means of a referee's throw.

The execution of the referee's throw shall be from the centre of the court by the court referee throwing the ball vertically into the air by a whistle signal. All the other players must be 3 m away from the referee while throwing. Two competing players shall stand either side of the referee. The referee shall throw the ball into the air and the two players shall jump to try and gain possession. The ball may be played after it has reached its highest point.

Skill

This is a rapid game of continuous action. It requires fitness and endurance as well as flexibility and balance. Passing, dribbling, and catching skills make a team perfect to possess the ball.

Skilful players can often carry the ball and defeat their opponent.

Netball

History

Netball is an interesting game of quick passing and shooting. This game was invented in America in 1890 and was introduced in England five years later. During the early stages of its development, the game was confined to certain groups of enthusiasts and there was no national importance attached to it. Netball was popular only among the students of physical training colleges of England. Very soon it attracted more followers and as it developed technically and became more specialized many modifications to the original rules were made and the amended rules were published in 1901.

Between 1901 to 1923 more schools and colleges started playing the game and many clubs and leagues were also organized. Despite the fact that netball was a foreign game, the British women took to it with a great deal of interest and in course of time preferred it to many other games. The International Federation of Basketball and Netball which came into existence in 1957 held an international conference in Ceylon. Certain important changes were made at this conference so that international tournaments and championships might be played under common rules. The All England Netball Association had the honour of holding the first international tournament in 1963.

Though this game was introduced in India by foreigners, it has became very popular in certain parts of the country. Inter-school and inter-collegiate matches are played in netball and the rules followed at present are the rules framed by the All-England Netball Association. Traditionally played by women, netball is fast becoming popular with both sexes.

The pitch

Netball is played on a firm surface, which is called 'pitch'. It is rectangular in shape and 100 ft long and 50 ft wide in size. The pitch is divided into three equal parts by marking two lines on it. A centre circle is marked of 4.9 metre in the centre of the pitch.

Equipments

Ball : The ball must be spherical and an association football size five. The circumference of the ball must be between 690 mm to 710 mm. The ball must consist the weight of 400 gm to 450 gm. It is made with leather, rubber or similar material.

Goalposts : Two goalposts are fixed at the mid point of each goal line. The goalposts are inserted into the ground in international matches. The posts are made of iron or steel and having the metal rings. The internal diameter of the ring is 380 mm. The attachment joining the ring and post must allow 150 mm between the post and the rear side of the ring. A net is fixed with the ring firmly.

Dress : Men wear shirt with shorts and women wear skirt and shirt. Initials of playing positions must be worn both front and back above the waist. The shoes must not have spiked soles and no jewellery may be worn except a wedding ring, which must be taped.

Teams

The match of netball is played between two teams. Each team consists of seven players with upto three substitutes. The playing positions are as under.
1. Goal shooter
2. Goal attack
3. Wing attack
4. Centre
5. Wing defence
6. Goal defence
7. Goalkeeper

Game

At the starting of a match the players take up their positions. The captain winning the toss chooses between taking the first centre pass or choosing an end. The centre of the team taking the first centre pass stands inside the centre circle. Apart from the centre and the opposition's centre, all the players must remain outside the centre third until the whistle blows. Goals are scored by the goal shooter sending the ball through the ring defended by their opponents, while standing within the goal circle.

Duration

A netball match consists of four quarters of 15 minutes each.

First quarter	—	15 minutes
Interval	—	3 minutes
Second quarter	—	15 minutes
Half time interval	—	10 minutes
Third quarter	—	15 minutes
Interval	—	3 minutes
Fourth quarter	—	15 minutes

A duration of two halves of 20 minutes each with an interval of 5 minutes is also permissible. This is more suitable for non-championship games.

Scoring a goal

A goal is scored when the ball is thrown or batted over completely through the ring by goal shooter or goal attack from any point within the goal circle including the lines bounding the goal circle. In taking a shot for goal a player shall have no contact with the ground outside the goal circle either during the catching of the ball or whilst holding it. It is not contact with the ground to lean on the ball, but if this happens behind the goal line the ball is considered to be out of court.

Throw-in

The throw-in is the act of putting the ball in play when the ball passes the side line or goal line and considered out. When the ball goes out of court, it is put into play by the opponent player who last touched it. The player throwing the ball must throw it into the adjacent third from behind the side lines. If after an unsuccessful shot at goal, the ball goes clearly out without being touched, the throw-in is made from any point along the part of the goal line which marks the goal circle.

Dos and don'ts

A player may:

(i)   Catch the ball with one or two hands.

(ii)   Gain or regain control of the ball if it rebounds from the goal post.

(iii)   Bat or bounce the ball to another player without first having possession of it. ·

(iv)   Tip the ball in an uncontrolled manner once or more than once.

(v)   Having batted the ball once, either catch the ball or direct the ball to another player.

(vi)   Roll the ball to oneself to gain possession.

(vii)   Fall while holding the ball but must regain footing and throw within three seconds of receiving the ball.

(viii)   Lean on the ball to prevent going offside.

(ix)   Lean on the ball on court to gain balance.

(x)   Jump from a position in contact with the court and play the ball outside the court.

A player may not:

(i)   Strike the ball with the fist.

(ii)   Deliberately fall on the ball to get it.

(iii)   Attempt to gain possession of the ball while lying, sitting or kneeling on the ground.

(iv)   Throw the ball while lying, sitting or kneeling on the ground.

(v)   Use the goalposts as a support in receiving the ball going out of the court.

(vi)   Use the goalposts as a means of regaining balance, or in any other way for any other purpose.

(vii)   Deliberately kick the ball.

Footwork

The rules allow larger freedom of movement. A player may receive the ball with both feet on ground and then step with either foot in any direction, lift the other foot and throw or shoot before this foot is placed on the ground again. He may step with either foot in any direction, any number of times, pivoting on the other foot. A player may lift the pivot foot, but must throw or shoot before he lands on that foot again. He may jump from both feet, but must throw or shoot before keeping either foot down on the ground.

A player may receive the ball when on foot or jump to catch and land on one foot and step with the other foot in any direction, lift the landing foot and throw or shoot before landing on that foot again. He can pivot on the landing foot and may lift the pivoting foot and throw or shoot before it is grounded. He may jump, but must throw the ball or shoot before either foot is regrounded.

Shooting

In a netball encounter the winners are decided by the number of goals scored during playing time and, therefore, accuracy in shooting is a very important factor. A natural aptitude for shooting is always a great asset, but above all an aptitude to learn and practise helps to produce very good results. One-handed 'running' shot, one-handed push shot and two-handed overhead shots are the kinds of shooting. With the help of regular practice for a period of at least 15 to 25 minutes a day is more value than infrequent practice periods. A shooter should be an advanced player who should be able to cope with interference and still shoot accurately, even in an off-balance position.

Obstruction

An attempt to intercept or defend the ball may be made by a defending player if the distance on the ground is not less than 0.9 metre from a player in possession of the ball. From the correct distance, a defending player may attempt to intercept or defend the ball by jumping towards the player with the ball, but if the landing is within 0.9 metre of that player and interferes with the throwing or shooting motion, obstruction occurs.

A player may be within 0.9 metre of an opponent in possession of the ball provided no effort is made to defend and there is no interference with that opponent's throwing or shooting action. From the correct distance, a defending player may not attempt to intercept or defend the ball by stepping towards an opponent with the ball. A player who is standing out of court may not attempt to defend a player who is on the court. A penalty pass or shot on the court will be awarded opposite the point where the infringement was standing.

Dodging

    (i)   Create a space by moving away from the player with the ball and move into the vacant space thus created.

   (ii) Run quickly in the direction of the goal and stop suddenly. The opponent may run on.

  (iii) Run fast in the direction of the ball, stop quickly and get back to receive the ball.

Different plans can be practised for getting the ball into the shooting circle before trying to use them in game. The effective pattern of passing the netball is zigzag. A set pattern of zigzag passing already planned and practised by a team will help to outwit the opposing team.

Skills

In netball, ball control depends on the ability to gather the ball and hold it safely until it is time for release. Every player should take pride in developing the skill needed for catching which is the most essential part of the game. Players of a team must feel confident that the ball will be held if it comes anywhere within easy or difficult reach. Players must also be able to throw firmly and swifty, also anticipating the speed and direction of the receiver. When a team is in attack, individual players must try to break free from their opponent and reach a clear strategic point from which to receive the ball and form a link down the court.

Judo

History

Judo is developed from an ancient Japanese method of unarmed combat known as *Jiujitsu*, also known as *Jujitsu*. It is a modern combat sport which is an amalgam of several old fighting arts. Judo has greatly advanced since 1882 when it was first devised by Dr. Jigoro Kano (1860-1938). He was the founder of 'Kodo Kan Judo' and designed the techniques of a new martial art i.e. judo to reflect the concept of maximum efficiency in the use of physical and mental energy.

The International Judo Federation was founded in 1951 and the first World Championships were inaugurated in 1956 in Tokyo. Judo was introduced in Olympics in 1964. The women championships were first held at New York in 1980. The International Judo Federation has more than 80 members from all over the world and it has grown into a full-fledged international sport. Not only in Japan and Korea or other eastern countries but also in the every heart of Europe this sport is greatly popular.

Competition area

The competition area is called judo ring, which must be a maximum of 16 metres square. It must be covered by a tatami or a similarly acceptable material. The competition area is divided into two zones. The area between these two zones is called 'danger zone'. This area is indicated by a red colour. It is approximately 1 metre wide, parallel to the four sides of the competition area. The area within and including the danger zone is called 'contest area'. The area outside the danger area is called 'safety area'. A red tape and a white tape must be fixed on the centre of the contest area 4 metre apart to indicate the positions at which the contestants must start and end the contest. The red tape must be to the referee's right and white to the referee's left.

Equipment

A few technical equipments are required for a contest:
— Two chairs for judges
— Red and white flag
— Two scoreboards
— Timing clock for contest duration and two for osaekomi
— Timekeeper's flag (yellow and blue)

Dress

The contestants must wear Judogi (Judo uniform) made of cotton or similar material. The Judogi must be in good condition and white or off-white or blue in colour. The jacket must be long enough to cover the thighs and reach at least

down to the fists when the arms are fully extended downwards. The trousers must be long enough to cover the legs and at their maximum reach to the ankle joint and at their minimum to 5 cm above the ankle joint. A strong belt of 4 to 5 cm wide must be worn over the jacket at waist level and tied with a square knot. The colour of the belt symbolises the grade the learner has passed.

Officials

The contest is governed by one referee and two judges. Referee generally remains within the contest area and conducts the bout. Before the start of a bout, the referee should ensure that the mat is clean, in good condition and that there is no gap between the mats. The referee shall make the required gesturers for indicating the scores, penalties stop and restart of the bout. While cancelling a score, there should be no announcement; only a gesture to that effect shall be sufficient. Referee calls '*Hantei*' at the end of the undecided contest. He adds his decisions and the result according to the majority ruling.

The judges sit opposite each other at two corners outside the contest area. Each should sit with both feet apart, on the mat. A judge should immediately express his opinion by way of the required gesture if he does not agree with the decision of a referee. If the referee does not notice the opinion of the judges, they should immediately stand up, maintain their gesture until the referee rectifies his evaluation. If the referee still does not pay attention to them, then the closest judge must immediately approach him and inform him of their opinion.

Categories

There are basically two categories – junior and senior category.

(i) Junior category (below 17 years of age)

Light weight	—	58 kg or less
Welter weight	—	58 kg to 64 kg
Middle weight	—	65 kg to 74 kg
Light-heavy weight	—	75 kg to 81 kg
Heavy weight	—	85 kg or more

(ii) Senior category (above 17 years of age)

Light weight	—	63 kg or less
Welter weight	—	63 kg to 69 kg
Middle weight	—	70 kg to 79 kg
Light-heavy weight	—	80 kg to 92 kg
Heavy weight	—	93 kg or above

Higher grades

The efficiency grades in Judo are divided into pupil (*kyu*) and master (*dan*) grades which have coloured belts in the following order:

9th *kyu*	—	Yellow belt
8th *kyu*	—	Orange belt
7th *kyu*	—	Orange belt
6th *kyu*	—	Green belt
5th *kyu*	—	Green belt
4th *kyu*	—	Blue belt
3rd *kyu*	—	Blue belt
2nd *kyu*	—	Dark tan or red belt
1st *kyu*	—	Dark tan or red belt

It is only after passing all the categories of *kyu* that one can be admitted to the degree course of *dan*. When a learner has learnt all the fundamental points of this sport, he is admitted to the 9th *kyu* and wears the customary yellow belt.

Dan grades are in the following order:

1st *dan*	—	Black belt
2nd *dan*	—	Black belt
3rd *dan*	—	Black belt
4th *dan*	—	Black belt
5th *dan*	—	Black belt
6th *dan*	—	Red and white belt
7th *dan*	—	Red and white belt
8th *dan*	—	Red and white belt
9th *dan*	—	Red belt
10th *dan*	—	Red belt
11th *dan*	—	Red belt
12th *dan*	—	Red belt

Starting

The contestants must stand facing each other on the contest area at the red or white tape according to the sash they are wearing. They must make a standing bow and take one step forward. The referee announces '*hajime*' to start the contest. The duration of the contest for world championship and Olympic games is five minutes for men and four minutes for women. A bell or similar audible device indicates to the referee the end of the time allotted for the contest. Contestants are entitled to rest for a period of ten minutes between the contest.

Osaekomi

It is awarded by the referee when a technique fulfils the following criteria:

(i)   When a contestant held by the other contestant is fully under control and must have his back, both shoulders or one in contact with the mat.

(ii)   The control can be from the rear, side or from top.

(iii) The legs of the contestant holding his opponent should not be controlled by his opponent.

(iv)   At least half of the contestant's bodies should be inside the contest area at the commencement of the *osaekomi*. The scores awarded on the basis of *osaekomi* are as under:

Ippon	—	Total of 30 seconds
Waza-ari	—	25 seconds or more but less than 30 seconds
Yuko	—	20 seconds or more but less than 25 seconds
Koka	—	10 seconds or more but less than 20 seconds

An *osaekomi* of less than 10 seconds shall be counted as an attack and no score shall be awarded. If *osaekomi* is announced simultaneously with the bell signal, the contest time shall be extended until announcement of *ippon*, *toketa* or *matte* by the referee.

Ippon

Ippon is achieved:

(i) When a contestant, with control, throws the other contestant largerly on his back with considerable force and speed.

(ii) When a contestant holds with *osaekomi* the other contestant, who is unable to get away for 30 seconds after the announcement of *osaekomi*.

(iii) When a contestant gives up by tapping twice or more with his hand or foot or says '*maitta*' (I give up), generally as a result of grappling technique, *shime-waza* (strangle) or *kansetsu-waza* (armlock).

(iv) When the effect of a strangle technique or armlock is sufficiently apparent.

(v) If one contestant gains two *waza-ari* in one contest, the contestant is awarded an *ippon* (called a '*waza-ari awasete ippon*').

Yuko

Yuko is awarded:

(i) When a contestant, with control, throws the other contestant, but the technique is partially lacking in two of the other three elements necessary for an *ippon*.

(ii) When a contestant holds with the *osaekomi* the other contestant who is unable to get away for 20 seconds or less than 25 seconds.

Matte

The contest may be temporarily halted, on the call of '*matte*' by the referee:

(i) If the contestants are about to leave the contest area

(ii) After any foul

(iii) If there is any illness or injury

(iv) To adjust the costume

(v) To disentangle unproductive holds

When the referee deems it necessary in any other case/ condition. After the announcement of '*matte*' the referee must ensure to maintain the contestants within has view, in case they do not hear the *matte* and continue fighting.

Koka

Koka is awarded:

(i) When a contestant, with control, throws the other contestant into his thigh (s) or buttocks with speed and force.

(ii) When a contestant holds with osaekomi the other contestant who is unable to get away for 10 seconds or more but less than 20 seconds.

Penalties

Like points, penalties are not cumulative. However, the awarding of a second or subsequent penalty automatically cancels an earlier penalty. When a contestant has already been penalized, any succeeding penalties must be awarded in higher value than the existing penalty. When a contestant is given a penalty, the opponent gains points.

Chui : It is awarded to any contestant who has committed a serious infringement or having been awarded a '*shido*' commits a second slight infringement. Serious infringement includes:

(1) To bend back the opponent's finger(s) in order to break the opponent's grip.

(2) To kick with the knee or foot, the hand or arm of the opponent in order to make the opponent release their grip.

Hansoku make : This award is given to a contestant who has committed a very grave infringement or, having been penalized for *keikoku*, commits a further infringement of any degree. Very grave infringement includes:

(i) Wearing a hard or metallic object.

(ii) Intentionally falling backwards when the opponent is clinging to the contestant's back and when either contestant has control of the other's movement.

Shido : A *shido* is given to any contestant who has committed a slight infringement. Slight infringement includes:

(i) To make an action designed to give the impression of an attack but which clearly shows that there was no intent to throw the opponent.

(ii) To put a hand, arm, foot or leg directly in the opponent's face.

Keikoku : *Keikoku* is awarded to any contestant who has committed a grave infringement or who has been penalized for *chui*, commits a further slight. Grave infringement includes:

(i) Making any action which might injure or endanger the opponent, or may be against the spirit of the game.

(ii) Disregarding the referee's instructions.

Skills

There are four key combat techniques used in Judo: *Nage-komi-waza* – throwing an opponent, *osaekomi-waza*—pinning an opponent to the ground, *kansetsu-waza* – armlocking an opponent and *shime-waza* – choking an opponent.

Kabaddi

History

The game of *Kabaddi* originated in India. So it can be called the basic game of India. This game is played in every state of India. During *Mahabharata* period, it was known by the name of 'one respiration'. It is known by different names in different parts — like '*Hu-du-du*' in Bengal, '*Hu-tu-tu*' in MP and Maharashtra, '*Chadugudu*' in *Tamil Nadu* and Karnataka.

Deccan Gymkhana published the rule book of *Kabaddi* in 1923. In 1934, Akhil Maharashtra Sharirik Parishad published the revised rules of *Kabaddi*. The first All India Kabaddi Championship was organised in 1938. Kabaddi was the demonstrated game in 1938 Berlin Olympics and it got the national level in 1951, when National Kabaddi Federation of India was founded. In 1957, Kabaddi was also demonstrated in the World Youth Festival at Moscow. In National Schools Games, Kabaddi was included in 1962 for boys and for girls in 1975. It was one of the demonstration games of 9th Asian Games played in 1982 at New Delhi.

Kabaddi is a very popular game in India, Pakistan, Burma, Sri Lanka, Nepal, Cambodia, Malaysia, Indonesia, Singapore, Thailand, Bangladesh etc.

Playground

The *Kabaddi* ground shall be a flat and soft-surfaced. It shall be made of earth, manure and sawdust. The dimension of the ground is different according to the categories:

Men	—	12 ½ metre × 10 metre
Women	—	11 metre × 8 metre
Junior / sub-junior	—	11 metre × 8 metre

The centre line divides the ground in two equal parts. Each of the strips on the side of the ground is known as lobby. The baulk-line shall be drawn though the entire width at a distance of 3.25 metre in the case of men and 2.5 metre in the case of women and men below 50 kg category. All the lines drawn must be 5 cm wide.

Dress

Every player is required to wear a T-shirt or *Sando* with shorts and footwear. The T-shirt has a number printed on it (4 inch long on front and 6 inch long on back). No one is allowed to wear any such thing which can injure the opponent or is against the rules of the game. The application of oil or any soft substances on the body or limbs is not allowed.

Game

Each team shall consist of 12 players including 5 substitutes. 7 players shall take the positions on the ground. The side that wins the toss shall have the choice of the court or the raid. The duration of the match shall be two halves of 20 minutes each in case of men and 15 minutes in case of women and men below 50 kg, with 5 minutes rest in the middle. The courts shall be changed after interval. The last raid of each half of the match shall be allowed to be completed even after completion of the scheduled time as mentioned above. The team scoring more points wins the game.

Officials

One referee, two umpires, one scorer and two assistant scorers are appointed to designate the game.

The decision of the umpires shall be final generally, but in special circumstances the referee may give his decision in the best interest of the game and when there is disagreement between the two umpires. The umpire shall conduct the whole match and give decisions according to the rules of the game. The referee shall take the toss, announce the score of each side at the end of each half and at the end of the match, supervise in general the conduct of the match, keep the time and shall start and end the game by his whistle, announce the substitution and replacement of any player.

The scorer shall fill the score sheet, all the points scored by any player of the team, time out by any team be indicated by 'T' against the team concerned and misc. jobs concerned to him. Assistant scorer shall keep record those who are out or their order of being out, revived and point out to the umpire if any player has gone out of bounds.

Features

(i)   A player shall be out if any part of his body touches the ground outside the boundary but during the struggle a player shall not be out if any part of his body touches directly the ground or any player who is inside the boundary.

(ii)   After the struggle is over, the players involved in the struggle may use the lobbies to enter their respective courts.

(iii)   Not more than one raider shall enter the opponent's court at a time.

(iv)   Player(s) out shall be revived in the game order as they were out when one or more opponent's are out.

(v)   If any raider is warned against any dangerous play or is in any way instructed by one of his own side, the umpire or referee shall award one point to the opponent.

(vi)   A maximum of 3 players can generally be substituted with the permission of the referee.

(vii)   No player shall instruct another in the course of play except the captain who may speak to his players in his own court only.

(viii) As long as a raider has not reached his court, none of the antis shall touch the ground of the raider's court beyond the midline with any part of his body. Otherwise he shall be out.

(ix)   A raider shall keep the cant with 'Kabaddi' as the word for sounding. If he is not keeping the cant he shall be ordered back and warned by the umpire and the opposing team will be given a chance to raid.

(x)   If any raider after warning, is purposely violating the rule of 'cant with Kabaddi', his turn shall be declared over and one point shall be awarded to the opposing team.

(xi)   Each side shall score one point for every opponent put out. The side which scores a 'Lona' shall score two points extra.

(xii) If any match is replayed, the players need to be the same again.

(xiii) Time-out may be called by the captain with the permission of the referee in the event of any injury to a player only.

(xiv) The time lost during the time-out period shall be added to the retaining time.

(xv) If a raider loses his cant in the opponent's court, he shall be out.

(xvi) After a raider has reached his court or is out in the opponent's court, the opponents shall send their raider within 5 seconds. Thus alternately each side shall send their raider until the end of the game.

(xvii) A raider or an anti is not be held by any part of his body deliberately other than his limb or trunk. The one who violates the rule first shall be declared out.

(xviii) Doping by player and officials shall not be allowed. Nails of the players must be closely clipped.

(xix) If a raider goes out of turn, he shall be ordered to go back and warned.

(xx) No anti shall wilfully push the raider out of the boundary by any part of his body, nor any raider shall wilfully push or pull any anti(s) out of the boundary.

(xxi) If owing to failure of light, heavy rain or any such disturbances a match is not completed, such match shall be played again. In case of temporary suspension, match will be continued.

(xxii) In the league system, the side that wins will score two league points and the loser will score zero point. In the case of a tie, both sides will score one league point each. If there is a tie in league points scored in the league system, the team(s) in the group will replay the match after drawing a lot and the matches so arranged will be decided on knock-out basis.

(xxiii) The team which scores the first leading point shall be declared the winner if the tie occurs at the end of the game of 50 minutes in case of men and 40 minutes in case of women and men below 50 kg.

Faults

(i)   To close the raider's mouth and breaks his cant.

(ii) Playing violating game.

(iii) Coaching by any player or coach from outside the court.

(iv) To make scissor grip to any raider.

Umpire uses the following cards in case of any fault:

Green card	—	Warning
Yellow card	—	Temporarily out of game for two minutes
Red card	—	Permanently out of game/ match

Golf

History

Golf is an interesting game like so many other sports. It is originated in Scotland during the Middle Ages, probably on the grassy dunes of Scotland's eastern coast. In 1457, King James-II of Scotland tried to ban his subjects from playing the game, because he felt that they were neglecting archery, a martial skill required to defend the realm.

During the 20th century it became popularised in U.S. An American player, Body Jones, invented some new shots to promote the game. At that time, it was known as *Pegnika* and later on as Golf.

In India, the game of golf was started by the British. The Royal Kolkata Golf Club is the oldest golf club in India. It was founded in 1829 and was renamed after the visit by King Edward-VII as Kolkata Golf Club. The Kolkata Ladies Golf Club was established by Mrs. Peddler in 1891. The nine-hole Gymchona golf course located in the lap of Kanchenjunga is at a height of 4,968 m. This is the highest golf course in the world.

The course

A golf ground is known as golf course. It consists 18 holes, although short 9-hole courses also exist. Each hole starts with a teeing ground. The whole golf course shall be covered with a smooth surface of grass and it must be well maintained. The surrounding should be of trees, rough grass, water features and sand bunkers which provide challenging obstacles to play.

The length of the golf course may be around 5500 to 7000 yards. Each hole should be indicated by a flag. The hole must be 4.25 inch in diameter and at least 4 inch deep.

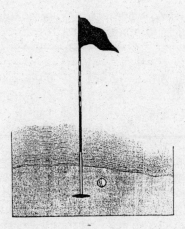

Equipments

Golf bag and golf cart : The golf bag stores clubs, balls and other accessories such as ball cleaner, pitch mark repairer, ball marker, towel, water bottle and some snacks. The bag can be attached to the cart. The cart is made of wood or steel which carries the accessories for ease of transport across the course.

Clubs : A club is used to hit the ball. Players take a set of clubs with them during the game. The club may be made of wood or iron. Each club has a different 'loft' or head angle, according to the required trajectory of the ball. The maximum number of clubs that a player is permitted to take on a ground of golf is 14. The types of clubs are as follows:

A) Wooden clubs

Number	Angle	Name
No. 1	12°	Driver – 109 cm long
No. 2	14°	Brossy
No. 3	16°	Spoon
No. 4	20°	Four wood
No. 5	24°	Five wood

B) Metal clubs

Numbers	Angle	Name
No. 2	19°	
No. 3	23°	Long iron
No. 4	27°	
No. 5	31°	

No. 6	35°	Middle iron
No. 7	39°	
No. 8	43°	Short iron
No. 9	47°	
Pitching ways	52°	89 cm long
Sand iron	58°	89 cm long

The ball : The balls come in a variety of materials, ranging from the inexpensive one-piece Surlyn ball to the more costly balata-covered ball with a liquid centre of yarn. The maximum weight of the ball must be 1.62 oz and the size should be 1.68 inch.

The tee : A peg is made of plastic or wood on which the ball is placed for the first stroke of each hole.

Game

Each hole starts at the teeing ground. The player strikes the ball with an appropriate club, selected for power or precision, aiming to land it on the green. The player then putts the ball into the hole. An 'ace', or hole-in-one is quite a rare feet. The game is played either by stroke play or match play. The score is calculated according to the total number of strokes made over the 18 holes in stroke play. In match play, the player's score indicates the number of holes they have won; a player wins a hole by completing it using fewer strokes than his competitors. A match is won by the side which is leading by a number of holes greater than the number of holes remaining to be played. For setting the tie, the stipulated round may be extended to as many holes as are required for a match to be won.

Officials

A marker records a competitor's score in stroke play. A fellow competitor may act as a marker. In competitions, a referee decides on questions of fact and applies the rules.

Behaviour

Golf has its own etiquette or code of behaviour. It is based on safety, honesty and consideration for follow players. The player should look around and behind before teeing off, to ensure that fellow-competitors or spectators will not be struck.

If the player is responsible for marking a score card, as is frequently the case in non-competition golf, he is honour bound to mark the card honestly and accurately.

Fellow competitors must not disturb a player who is about to strike the ball, either by talking or by making any other noise or movement.

Terms

The following terms are associated with golf:

Backspin : Spinning motion imparted to a well-played stroke to the green.

Hook : Faulty stroke in which the ball swerves to the left when played by a right-handed player.

Putting green : The prepared area ground the hole containing the flagstick. An 18-hole golf course has 18 putting greens.

Local rules : Special rules made by a club committee to meet local conditions, but which are not contrary to the rules of the game.

Slice : To hit a ball so that it travels in an arc to the right in the case of a right-handed player.

Hazard : Any permanent obstacle like bunker, water hazard that may impede a player's progress round the course.

Obstruction : Anything artificial, erected, placed or left on the course; railings, walls, rads, paths, bridge supports or any construction declared by the committee to be an integral part of the course.

Push-stroke : Stiff-armed stoke with little wrist movement designed to keep the flight of the ball below the normal trajectory.

Advice : Guidance, other than on rules or local, which may be provided during the game only by a partner or caddie.

Caddie : One who carries a player's clubs during and assists in accordance with the rules of the game.

Waggle : The movements made by the player between taking up his stance and making a stroke.

Borrow : Allowance in direction made in putting on an undulating surface; on a level surface there is no borrow.

Divot : Piece of turf removed in playing a stroke.

Bye : Hole or holes remaining to be played after a match has been decided.

Heel : The part of a club-head which touches the ground when the stance is taken up; also to hit the ball with this part of the club.

Niblick : Steel-headed club formerly with a wooden shaft, now with a steel shaft and known as No.7 or No.8 iron.

Par : Number of strokes for a round or hole assessed by the standard scratch score fore the course.

Lie : Position in which ball comes to rest.

Gymnastics

History

The origin of gymnastics is somewhat obscure. But it is believed that around 2600 B.C. the Chinese people developed some activities concerned with *yoga* which resembled with gymnastics. The actual development of gymnastics began in the early Greek and Roman periods. The Greek first gave great emphasis to gymnastics, in fact, the word *Gymnastics* itself is derived from Greek.

Johann Basedow of Germany added gymnastics exercises to the programme of instructions in his schools in 1776. Johann Guts Muths is known as the "great grandfather" of the game. He introduced gymnastics in various schools and other institutions.

Another person, who gave a great contribution to promote gymnastics, is Schripilng. His student H. Ling used to promote this game in the countries of America, Denmark, Germany etc. after the death of Schripilng. During 1850, it became a popular game worldwide. It was introduced in Olympics in 1966.

Floor

The floor exercise must form a harmonious and rhythmical whole alternating among movements of the gymnastics and tumbling elements. Available floor must be of 12 x 12 metres in all directions should be used, and the gymnast may not step out of this area. The duration of the floor exercise is 50 to 70 seconds.

Special requirements:
(i)   Three tumbling connections with at least 1 c – part.
(ii) One strength part, at least of B-value and one hold part (balance or hold parts on one leg or one arm).

Apparatus
Pommel horse : The exercise must be composed

exclusively of clean swings without steps. Double leg circles with feet together must be predominant, and the gymnast during the performance of an exercise must use all three parts of the horse. He must show flowing movements that travel up and down the apparatus.

Rings : The exercise on ring must be composed in about equal proportions between swing, strength and hold parts, which can be arranged in any variation, but during the hold and strength parts of rings must be still. Every competitor first performs the current compulsory exercise as laid down by the FIG. The element comprising the compulsory exercise are of the same general kind as for the optional exercise.

Vaulting : Judging in this event is somewhat different than in others. In this, the gymnast may perform twice, the

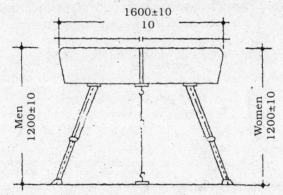

higher score counting in his total and lower one being is disregarded.

Parallel bars : The parallel bars should be stable enough and uprights must prevent vibrations during an exercise. On placing weight of 136 kg in the middle of each bar, it

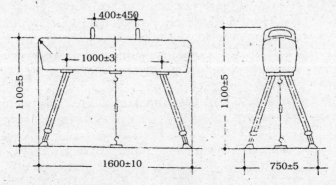

should cause a sag of 60 mm with a tolerance of 6 mm up or down; on removal of the weight it must resume its original shape. The parallel bars offer the gymnast an infinite variety of movements and combinations. The exercise must consist of swinging parts, hold parts and movements with release and regrasps over and under the bars. Strength and exercise parts performed sideways can also be demonstrated. The exercise may not contain more than three 2-second hold parts.

Horizontal bar : The high or horizontal bar consists of a bar of stainless steel 28 mm diameter and 2400 mm in length, upright made of steel pipes, steel wires, floor anchors and chains made of steel. The horizontal bar exercise must be composed exclusively of swinging parts without stop and movements where the body is brought close to the bar. Further more, the exercise may consist of giant swings.

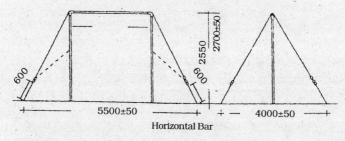

Horizontal Bar

Side Horse vaulting : This apparatus is specially for women. Women vault with the horse turned across the run-up. Women have no limit to the distance they can take for their run, although most prefer at least 20 metres. A woman gymnast can attempt each vault twice, but only the higher of the two scores counts. She can choose from 59 kinds of vault in eight different groups. She must indicate to the judges the vault she is performing before she starts her run. All gymnasts may invent new moves. In vaulting, top performers sometimes add an extra turn to an existing vault to gain a higher mark. A minimum distance of 20 metres, including a spring hold, must be provided for the run up.

Uneven parallel bars (Asymmetric bars) : This apparatus is used by female gymnasts. They use it to swing their bodies and change their hand grasps from bar to bar. In this event, as on the balance beam, a large quantity of difficult elements is not desirable, as they hinder the performance of a measured and assured exercise. Here, movement is important, and should be almost continuous. Static positions may be only momently and should be avoided whenever possible. A maximum of two stops during an exercise is allowed, but only if the stops are in balance.

Balancing beam : The balancing beam consists of a steel base and a 5000 mm long and 100 mm wide beam. The whole beam shall be covered with a tear-proof, hygroscopic material having good grip. Balance and rhythm, rather than a number of difficult stunts, are what judges look for in this event. The rules of the beam exercise are as usual, found in the code of points. The exercise must contain acrobatic elements with forward and backward movements, full turns (one on one leg), walking steps, running steps, jumps and leaps. The gymnast must perform smoothly on the whole length of the beam and must introduce changes of rhythm.

Dress

Men : Men must wear a shirt (jersey) in all events. In the events performed on the pommel horse, rings, parallel bars and horizontal bar, men must wear long white pants and footwear. The same dress may be worn for the floor exercise and vault or else short pants with or without footwear. In competition 1 the member of a team must wear uniform clothing of same colour, but an individual's choice of long or short pants for all the exercise and vault is unaffected.

Women : Women wear leotards, the precise cut of which may be varied to suit a particular event provided the general appearance remains essentially unchanged. Securely

fastened bandages are allowed, but padding is prohibiled. The wearing of gymnastic slippers and socks is optional. In competition 1 the members of a team must wear identical leotards.

Scoring

Each gymnast's performance on each apparatus is marked on the scale 0-10. Each judge, including the head judge, assesses the gymnast's performance in strict accordance with the standards and points of reference laid down by the FIG. In some events there is a starting score, with a possible bonus for risk, originality and virtuosity which together make up the maximum possible of 10. Bonus points can be earned by the demonstration of risk and originally in the B and C parts. For additional D-elements a maximum of 0.10 points will be given, that means:

— In competition I B   — One D - element
— In competition II   — One D - element
— In competition III   — More than one D - element

Bonus points for D will be given for the successful D-element/connections.

Jury

For meets of the FIG, Olympic Games, international competitions, continental or regional meets, the jury for each consists of five men, namely: one superior judge and four judges, from the list of international judges, who are nominated by member organizations which take part in the competition.

Duties of judges

(i)   The judges have the duty to attend the judges courses and all scheduled meetings for the competitions for which they have been selected and seeded by the TC/FIG to participate, and are to arrive punctually according to the time and directions in the work plan.

(ii)   The judge has the right to file a written protest with the director of the competition in case of arbitary action taken against him by the superior judge.

(iii) The judges serving at an apparatus are to adhere to all parts of the code of points, possible written instructions of the TC/FIG, instructions obtained at judges courses and the instructions of the superior judge, and are completely responsible for the scores they award.

(iv) To perform their duties, they must possess the code of points, as well as any special material issued by the TC/FIG. Otherwise they can be replaced by the directors of the competition. The officers of the federation involved assume full responsibility.

(v) Judges who do not take sufficient interest in meetings, or are absent or appear late for courses and meetings, can be replaced by the director of the competition.

Terms

Floor –

(i) *Arabersprung* **(Arabian cartwheel)** : Free cartwheel sideward, body bent forward with ½ turn around longitudinal axis, from straddle stand.

(ii) **Japanese jump** : From stand arms upward : lowering arms forward and jump in place lowering arms forward downward with ¼ turn or ½ turn around the longitudinal axis of body to support and front leaning support or handstand.

(iii) *Thomas* : Jump backward with 1½ turn and 1½ salto forward tucked or picked to roll.

(iv) Li Yuejiu : 1½ salto sideways with straddle and ¼ turn to roll.

Pommel horse –

(i) *Chaguinian* : From support rearways at left end of horse : flank right backward with ¼ turn right and change of support right on left end of horse and ¼ turn right to flank left with change of support left on left end of horse. Double leg circle, 1½ and 2 times ¼ turn right to support earways on left end of horse. Flank right backward with ¼ turn right and change of support right on left end of horse to wende swing left and dismount to outer cross stand right.

(ii) Magyar Travels : Travel circles in cross support over

entire horse with support on the three parts of the horse and on the pommels.

(iii) Magyar Spindle : Double leg circles with ½ turn around longitudinal axis in cross support at the end of horse, followed by double leg circles with ½ longitudinal turn w.o.i.c.

(iv) Russian Wende : From double leg circle in support front ways wende to left with ¼ turn left support frontways on opposite side of horse.

(v) Russian Wende-Swings : From double leg circles in support frontways, wende to left with ¼ turn right and wende to left with ¼ turn right with corresponding change of support to support frontways on the same side of horse.

(vi) Schwabenflanke : From support rearways on the left end of the horse: flank right backward with ¼ turn right and support change right on left end of horse and ¼ turn right to flank left with support right and support change left on the left pommel.

(vii) Stockli : From support frontways on the pommels : double leg circle left with ½ turn right and support right to momentary support rearways on right end of the horse, double leg circle right 1½ times with ½ turn right and support right to support rearways on the pommels.

(viii) Stockli Backward : From support rearways on the pommels : double leg circle right with ½ turn right and support left with change of support right on left end of horse to flank left in support rearways on the left end of horse.

(ix) Direct Stockli (A) : From support frontways on pommels : double rear vault swing around right arm to cross support rearways on right pommel, flank swing right backward with ¼ turn right to support frontways on pommels.

(x) Direct Stockli (B) : From support frontways on pommels double rear vault swing around right arm to cross support rearways on right pommel, flank swing right backward with ¼ turn right to support frontways on right pommel.

(xi) Suisse Simple : Front support frontways on the pommels : cut the right leg outward and ½ turn left with hop and change of grip, right hand on left pommel and left hand on right pommel, Out right leg outward to support rearways.

(xii) Suisse Double : From support forntways on the pommels : flank right and ½ turn left with hop and change of support, left hand on right pommel and right hand on left pommel to double leg circles.

(xiii) Tramlot : Front support rearways on pommels : double leg travel circles right to support rearways on left end of the horse, flank right backward and double leg circle with ½ turn right around right arm and change of support on right pommel to support rearways on the pommels.

(xiv) Tramlot Direct : From support rearways on pommels: flank right backward with change of support right on left pommel and double leg circle left with ½ turn right around right arm and change of support left on right pommel to support rearways on the pommels.

(xv) Tshechenkehre: From support rearways on pommels: double leg circle right 1½ times with ¼ turn right around left arm and change of support right on left pommel, reverse grip and ¼ turn right around right arm and change of support left on right pommel to support rearways on the pommels.

(xvi) Tshechenkehre Straddled : From support frontways on pommels : leg cut right outward and swing left to momentary side support over left pommel. ¼ turn right and leg right outward and change of support right on left pommel, reverse grip rear vault left with ¼ turn right to support rearways on the pommels.

(xvii) Czechwende : From support rearways on pommels: double leg circle right and ¼ turn right around left arm and change of support right on left pommel, reverse grip and ¼ turn right around right arm with change of support left on support frontways on the pommels.

(xviii) Mikolay : Triple direct stockli B w.o.i.c.

Rings –

(i) Streuli : Forward swing in hang and circle upward swing to handstand.

(ii) Honma : Rearward swing in hang and bent inlocate forward to felge rearward and backward swing to support.

(iii) Guczoghy : Double felge tucked backward swing in hang.

(iv) Li Ning : Felge upward rearward, backward and Stemme to left support.

Parallel Bars –

(i) Diamidov-Turn : Swing forward in support and 1/1 turn left with support on left arm through handstand to swing forward in support.

(ii) Healy-Twirl : Backward swing in support and 1/1 left turn around left arm through momentary handstand to backward swing in support.

(iii) Hurzeler : Diamidov-turn with subsequent quarter turn to side handstand or one rail and straddle dismount.

(iv) Japanese Salto : Rearward swing in upper arm hang and back uprise followed by salto forward to rearward swing in support.

(v) Carminucci on Parallel Bars : Swing forward in support with 1/1 turn around longitudinal axis of body to swing backward in upper arm hang.

(vi) Schwabenkippe : Forward swing in support and lower backward to bent inverted hand and hop to swing backward in upper arm hang or support or with ½ turn to swing forward in upper arm hang.

(vii) Slide kip : Forward swing in hang holding legs forward upward and cast to support or with ½ turn to forward swing in upper arm hang.

(viii) Guschiken : From handstand : forward swing to hang and salto backward with ½ turn to upper arm hang.

(ix) Richard : Stemme forward and diamidov-turn.

(x) Li Ning : From handstand : Giant backward with ½ turn to support.

(xi) Zellweger : From side handstand : forward swing to hang salto backward with straddle to side stand rearways.

(xii) Peters : Salto backward with ¼ turn to side handstand on one bar.

(xiii) Watanabe : Roll backward with ½ turn to upper arm support.

Horizontal bar –

(i) Koste : Czech uprise with stoop out backward.

(ii) Endoshoot : From handstand : lower forward to momentary straddle left support or stoop through momentary support rearways and free straddle or stoop forward to handstand, reverse grip.

(iii) Straumann Backward : Giant swing backward and before coming to handstand, salto backward tucked over the bar to side stand frontways : C.

(iv) Straumann Forward : Giant swing forward and before arriving in handstand, salto forward tucked over the bar to side stand rearways : C

(v) Russian Giant Swing : Giant swing forward in reverse grip and hang rearways.

(vi) Straldershoot : From hand stand or free hip circle : lower to momentary free straddle left support or stoop through to free support rearways and free hip circle backward to handstand.

(vii) Czeck Giant Swing : Giant swing backward in hang rearways.

(viii) Czeck Uprise : From support rearways : Overhead swing backward in hang rearways and uprise to free support rearways.

(ix) Jager : From giant swing forward : backward swing in hang salto forward straddled or closed legs to forward swing in hang.

(x) Kova-CS : From giant swing backward : 1½ salto backward to hang.

(xi) Gaylord : From giant swing forward : ½ salto forward to hang.

(xii) Deltschev : From giant swing backward : forward swing in hang and salto backward straddled with ½ turn to forward swing in hang.

(xiii) Gienger : From giant swing backward : forward swing in hang and salto backward picked with ½ turn to forward swing in hang.

(xiv) Winkler : From giant swing forward : backward swing in hang and salto forward with ½ turn hang.

(xv) Deff : From giant swing backward : forward swing in hang and salto backward with 1½ turn to forward swing in hang.

(xvi) Katschov: From giant swing backward: torward swing in hang and backward straddled over bar and regrasp to forward swing in hang.

(xvii) Suarez : On one arm grant backward with ½ turn and salto forward with straddle to forward swing in hang.

(xviii) Cuervo : From one arm giant : Straddle backward to hang.

(xix) Piatti-Salto : Free hip circle backward to momentary handstand and salto forward picked with straddle to forward swing in hang : C

Uneven Bar –

(i) Clear hip circle to a handstand : Clear hip circle to a handstand (2 x recognition as a value part).

(ii) Stalder backward to handstand : Clear hip circle to a handstand (third clear hip circle : no recognition as value part).

Balance Beam –

(i) Flic-Flac – A : Walkover backward (recognition of both value parts).

(ii) Flic-Flac – B : Salto backward with step out (recognition of both value parts).

(iii) Flic-Flac – C : Salto backward tucked (third flic-flac : no recognition as value part).

Archery

History

The history of English archery comes to us over the years. From the very earliest days when the crude bow and flint arrow-head provided our ancestors with their food, through the Middle Ages when the English bowman was supreme on the battlefields of Europe and when the use of bow was compulsory for all able-bodied men, to the present day when it is the sport and relaxation of thousands of men and women throughout the country.

Today archery is governed in Great Britain by the G.N.A.S. (Grand national Archery Society) which, through its constituent regional societies and in turn their affiliated country associations covers the whole of the U.K. except Scotland. Archery with bows and arrows developed as a pastime in the 16th century after the decline of the bow as a weapon.

Modern Archery is practised mostly in the form of target shooting. A number of clubs and institutions have special facilities to promoting the game specially in youngsters.

Game

In archery, most tournaments are held for individual competitors only though there are also team matches. An archer's main opponent, besides the wind and weather, is himself – his mental and physical conditions and any carelessness in keeping his own tackle in perfect order. There are following kinds of shooting:

Target archery : Target archery is the most famous kind of the game. It is played in many parts of the world, specially in Great Britain. Targets are set up at one end of the ground and rounds of a predetermined number of arrows are shot from one or more fixed distances.

Field archery : This attracts a large number of people in some countries, specially in U.K. A series of targets is set up at varying distances over a considerable area of health or woodland, up hill and down dale, to simulate conditions found in hunting. Competitors completes the round by shooting target to target.

Rovers : This is somewhat similar, but here a small group of archers roams around together, preferably over pasture land, shooting one or two arrows at any mark that happens to take their fancy – a molehill or tree stump the nearest arrow to each mark scoring one point.

Clout shooting : Clout shooting is similar to ordinary target shooting, but is at distances approaching the extreme range of bow so that arrows fly to a considerable height and drop into the target marked out flat on the ground.

Flight shooting : It has the small body of facilities perhaps the most important and thrilling of all kinds. This is for distance only. The importance to archery as a whole may be likened to that of racing to touring cars in the development of design and materials.

Equipment

A newcomer to the archery is most strongly advised not to buy bows or arrows until he has received personal advice about it from an expert. Most clubs keep some tackle suitable for a beginner to learn the rudiments of shooting with, and will be only too pleased to give a possible recruit a chance to find out whether he really would enjoy becoming an archer. Here are some necessary equipments for archery.

Bow : There are three main types of bow to choose from:

(i) Plain Wooden : These are mainly suitable for short distances.

(ii) Steel : These are probably the most economical in terms of efficiency for money and are used by many top-class archers.

(iii) Laminated : Laminated or composite bows constructed in combinations of wood for the core and various types of plastic and fibreglass on the belly and back.

Bow is usually 5 to 6 ft. long. From the fact that some of these composite bows cost from twice to four times as much as the simpler types of steel bow it may be safely guessed that they possess shooting qualities specially speed and smoothness not found in other bows. Weight of bow for men is 36 to 45 pounds and for women 24 to 30 pounds.

Arrow : Arrows must be matched within small limits to the bow from which they are to be shot. This will result a good shooting. Arrows that are too stiff or too whippy for the bow will never allow the archer to achieve the best result. Arrow is composed of a wooden or metal shaft and feathered flights. The length of arrow for men is 26 to 28 inch and for women 24 to 26 inches.

Bracer : The bracer is a guard made of leather which is worn on the arm holding the bow to protect it against bruising by the bowstring.

Glove : The shooting glove is worn on the 'Shaft hand' – the one which draws the string – may be an actual glove with reinforced tips for the first three fingers or finger-stalls attached to a skeleton glove, or it may be more commonly used 'tab' which is a piece of flat leather.

Standing

Archer's left shoulder should be towards the target. He should feel comfortable at the stand-at-ease position across the shooting line, about 6 to 9 inches apart, so that lines through the heels and shoulders will be squarely right distributed on both feet. The bow should be held gently with the knuckle at the base of the thumb towards the string, so that, when the string is drawn back, the weight of the bow is taken against the pad at the base of the thumb.

Nocking

The arrow is not held onto the string or drawn back directly with the finger. The point on the string opposite the arrow-rest is built up with thread or adhesive tape for a distance of about a quarter inch above that point so as to fit into the arrow nock snugly, but not so tightly as to risk splitting the nock, so that when the string is drawn back it takes the arrow with it.

Drawing

Generally archers used three fingers for drawing the string, though just a few archers use only two fingers. The first finger is hooked on the first joint above, but not touching the arrow and the next two fingers together below the arrow.

When the string is fully drawn back, the fingers will inevitably close up on the arrow, but an arrow which is tightly pinched between the fingers will almost invariably wobble in flight. Hence the reason for starting the draw with the fingers clear of the arrow, leaving the string properly fitting the nock to pull the arrow back.

Holding

Holding is the brief pause at full draw while the aim is perfected. During it and right up to the instant of loosing there must be no relaxing of the pull and push that would allow the arrow to creep forward. The point of the arrow can be aimed at a natural or artificial mark on the ground between the archer and the target. At short distances, this 'point-of-aim' may be nearer to the archer than the target and with good equipment will still be below the target at the longest distances normally shot at competitions. The other way is to use a 'sight' or mark on the bow above the arrow, often a strip of sticky tape, which is lined up with the target. The higher it is on the bow, the farther the bow-hand will be depressed for short ranges, and the nearer the mark is to the hand the farther the arrow will fly if the mark is again lined up with the target.

Boxing

History

The history of boxing is littered with blood yet it is very much a game and should be played in the spirit only. It has a long and chequered history as a game. There are references of '*Maushtic Yudha*' or '*Fist-Fight*' in *Mahabharata* and *Ramayana*. The physical bouts in those times included wrestling and boxing in a combined form. Even in ancient Greece boxing was reckoned to be an important game and Thesius was the uncrowned king during that period. In modern times, too, boxing is a very popular game owing to the tantrums exhibited by its great exponents.

Boxing with gloves was depicted on a fresco from the Isle of Thera, Greece, which has been dated 1520 B.C. The earliest prize-ring code of rules were formulated in England on 16th August 1743 by the champion pugilist Jack Broughton (1704 – 89) who reigned from 1734 to 1750. Boxing which had in 1867 came under the Queensberry Rules formulated for John Sholto Doughlas, 8th Marquess of Queensberry (1844 – 1900), was not established as a legal sport in Britain until after the ruling of R. Roberts and others of Mr. Justice Grantham, following the death of Billy Smith due to a fight on 24 April 1901.

Boxing was included in the Olympic Games in 1904. It was introduced in Asian Games in 1954. In 1949, the Boxing Federation of India was founded which organized the first National Championship in 1950 in Mumbai.

The Ring

The boxing ring shall be 16 ft square minimum and 20 ft. square maximum inside the lines of the ropes. It shall not be less than 3 ft. or more than 4 ft above the ground or base. The floor shall be covered with felt, rubber or other suitable approved material. Over it the canvas shall be stretched and

secured in place. The felt, rubber and other approved material, and canvas shall cover the entire platform. The platform shall be constructed safely and free from any obstructing projections. Four corner posts shall be fitted in four corners which shall be well padded. It should also be provided with suitable steps.

Equipments

Ropes : There shall be three ropes of a thickness of 1.18 inch minimum to 1.96 inch maximum drawn from the corner posts at 1 ft 3.7 inches, 2 ft 7½ inches and 4 ft 3 inches high respectively. The ropes shall be covered with a soft or smooth material and shall be joined on each side at equal intervals by two pieces of close textured canvas 1½ inch wide. The pieces must not slide along the ropes.

Gloves: Each boxer is used to fight with two gloves (to be worn on each hand). The gloves shall each weigh 8 ounces of which the leather portion shall not weigh more than 4oz and the padding not less than 4oz. The regular hitting surface be marked on the gloves with a clearly discernible colour. The padding of the gloves shall not be broken or displaced. The laces shall be tied on the outside of the back of the wrist of the gloves. Only clean and serviceable gloves shall be used for the contests.

Bandages : A soft surgical bandage, not to exceed 8 ft 4 inch in length and 2 inch in width or a bandage of the Velpeau type not to exceed 6 ft 6 inch in length on each hand may be worn. No other kind of bandage may be used. The use of any kind of tapes, rubber or adhesive plaster as bandage is strictly forbidden, but a single strap of adhesive 3 inch long and 1 inch wide may be used at the upper wrists to secure the bandages.

Ring Equipment : Two shallow trays containing ground resin; two seats (stools); two swilling seats for boxer's use during intervals between the rounds; two water bottles and two mugs; two basins with sawdust; gong or bell; one stop-watch; pads or printed score sheets; first-aid box; slotted lockable box; microphone connected to the loudspeaker system; towel and sponge for the boxer.

Dress

Both boxers shall be dressed as required by the governing body. Boxers shall box in light boots or shoes, shorts reaching at least half-way down the thigh, and a vest covering the chest and back. Where trunks and vests are of the same colour the belt line must be clearly indicated by a distinctive colour. Gum shields may be worn and a cup protector shall also be worn. A jockstrap may be worn in addition.

Officials

One referee, five judges and one timekeeper are appointed for a contest. The whole contest shall be controlled by the referee who shall officiate in the ring, but shall not mark a scoring paper. The five judges shall be seated separate from public and immediately adjacent to the ring. Two of the judges shall be seated on the same side of the ring at a sufficient distance from one another, and each of the three judges shall be seated at the centre of one of the other three sides of the ring – Timekeeper shall strike the gong to stop the bout if the referee is incapacitated in the course of a bout. His main duty is to regulate the number and duration of the rounds and the interval between the rounds. He shall be seated directly at the ring side. He shall commence and end each round by striking the gong. He shall also regulate all periods of time and counts by watch. At a 'knock-down' he shall signal to the referee with his hand the passing of the seconds while the referee is counting.

Classification of weight:

1.	Light fly	up to 48 kg (106 Ib)
2.	Fly	over 48 kg and up to 51 kg. (112 Ib)
3.	Bantam	over 51 kg and up to 54 kg (111 Ib)
4.	Feather	over 54 kg and up to 57 kg (126 Ib)
5.	Light	over 57 kg and up to 60 kg (132 Ib)
6.	Light welter	over 60 kg and up to 63.5 kg (140 Ib)
7.	Welter	over 63.5 kg and up to 67 kg (148 Ib)
8.	Light middle	over 67 Kg and up to 71 kg (157 Ib)
9.	Middle	over 71 kg and up to 75 kg (165 Ib)
10.	Light heavy	over 75 kg and up to 81 kg
11.	Heavy	over 81 kg and up to 91 kg (179 Ib)
12.	Super heavy	over 91 kg (201 Ib)

Weigh-in

All contestants must weigh-in, stripped on the day of the competition. It shall be the power of the executive committee to relax this condition slightly if avoidable delay occurs. The weigh-in shall be effected by the officials nominated by the organizers. The competitor will be allowed to present himself at the official scales only once at the weigh-in each day. The weight recorded on that presentation is final. It is permissible, however, for the delegate of any competitor who has failed to make the weight at the original weigh-in to enter him there upon for the higher weight for which he is qualified if such organization has a free place at that weight. The competitor shall be provided with a card upon which shall be entered the decision of the appointed doctor of medicine and by the appointed official the fact that he has duly weighed-in.

Draws and byes

The draw shall take place after the medical examination and weigh-in. It must take place in the presence of official, representatives of the teams. The draw shall proceed first for the boxers to box in the first series and then for the byes. However, no boxer may be awarded a world championship medal without having boxed.

In competitions where there are more than four competitors, a sufficient number of byes shall be drawn in the first series to reduce the number of competitors in the second series to 4, 8, 16 or 32. Competitors drawing a bye in the first series shall be the first to box in the second series. If there is an odd number of byes, the boxer who draws the last bye will complete in the second series against the winner of the first bout in the first series. Where the number of bouts is even, the boxers drawing byes shall box the first bouts in the second series in the order in which they are drawn. No medal shall be awarded to a boxer who has not boxed at least once.

Rounds

Bouts consist of five rounds of two minutes each, with a one-minute interval between rounds. Some international contests may consist of three or four rounds of three minutes each or six rounds of two minutes each. No additional round will be given.

Points

The points shall be awarded as per the following system:

(i) Concerning hits

During each round a judge shall assess the respective scores of each boxer according to the number of hits obtained by each. Each hit to have scoring value must, without being blocked or guarded, land directly with the knuckle part of the closed glove of either hand on any part of the front or sides of the head or body above the belt. Swing landing as above described are scoring hits.

The value of hits scored in a rally of fighting shall be assessed at the end of such rally and shall be credited to the boxer who has hit better of the exchange according to the degree of superiority.

The hits are not scoring hits if they are struck by a boxer while infringing any of rules; with the side, heel, inside of the glove or with the open glove, with any part of the glove other than the knuckle part of the closed glove; which land on arms or which merely connect without the weight of the body or shoulder.

(ii) Concerning Fouls

During each round a judge shall assess the seriousness and shall impose a suitable scoring penalty for any foul witnessed by him irrespective of the fact whether the referee has observed a foul or not.

If the referee warns one of the competitors, the judges may award a point to the other competitor. When a judge decides to award a point to a competitor for a foul committed by his opponent, he shall place a 'W' in the appropriate column against the points of the warned competitor to show that he has done so. If he decide not to so award a point, he shall in the appropriate column place the letter 'X' against the points allotted for that round to the warned competitor.

If a judge observes a foul apparently unnoticed by the referee and imposes an appropriate penalty on the offending competitor, he shall indicate that he has done so by placing in the appropriate column the letter 'J' against the points of the offending competitor, and indicating the reason why he has done so.

(iii) Concerning the award of points

There are 20 points that shall be awarded in each round. No fraction of points may be given. At the end of each round the better boxer shall receive 20 points and his opponent proportionately less. In the case of equal, each shall receive 20 points. If at the end of the contest and having marked each round in accordance with directive (i) and (ii), a judge shall find that the boxers are equal in points, he shall award the decision to the boxer who has done most of the leading off or has shown better who has done most of the leading off or has shown better style if equal, in that respect; who has shown better defence by which the opponent's attacks have been made to miss.

Fouls

(i)   Hitting below the belt, holding, tripping, kicking and butting with foot or knee.

(ii)   Ducking below the belt of the opponent in a manner dangerous to his opponent.

(iii)   Hitting with open glove, the inside of the glove, wrist or side of the hand.

(iv)   Useless, aggressive or offensive utterances during the round.

(v)   Pivot blows.

(vi)   Attempting to strike the opponent immediately after the referee has ordered 'Break' and before taking a step back.

(vii)   Lying on, wrestling and throwing in the clinch.

(viii)   Spitting out gumshield.

(ix)   Holding the opponent.

(x)   Holding and hitting or pulling and hitting.

(xi)   Completely passive defence by means of double cover and intentionally falling to avoid a blow.

(xii)   Hits or blows with head, shoulder, forearm, elbow, throttling of the opponent, pressing with arm or elbow in opponent's face, pressing the head of the opponent back over the ropes.

(xiii)   Not stepping back when ordered to break.

(xiv)   Hits landing on the back of the opponent and specially any blow on the back of the neck or head and kidney punch.

(xv)   Assaulting or behaving in an aggressive manner towards a referee at any time.

(xvi)   Attack whilst holding the ropes or making any unfair use of the ropes.

(xvii)   Keeping the advanced hand straight in order to obstruct the opponent's vision.

(xviii)   Attack on an opponent who is down or who is in the act of rising.

Down

A competitor shall be considered down if he touches the floor with any part of his body other than his feet as a result of a blow or series of blows; if he hangs helplessly on the ropes as a result of blows or series of blows; if he is outside or partly outside the ropes as a result of a blow or series of blows; if following a hard punch he has not fallen and is not lying on the ropes, but is in a semi-concious state and cannot, in the opinion of the referee, continue the bout.

In the case of knock-down, the referee shall immediately begin to count the seconds. When a boxer is down the referee shall count aloud from one to ten with intervals of a second between the numbers.

If a boxer is down, his opponent must at once go to neutral corner as designated by referee.

When a boxer is down as a result of a blow, the bout shall not be continued until the refereee has reached the count of eight, even if the boxer is ready to continue before then.

After referee has said 'ten' and the word 'out', the bout ends and shall be decided as a 'knock-out'.

Winning

Most contests are decided on points – that is, on points awarded to each boxer by the judges up to the end of the contest. Only rarely a bout is decided by a knockout. There are mainly following kinds of decisions, with which a boxer may win:

(i) Winning by points:

At the end of a contest the boxer who has been awarded the decision by a majority of the judges, shall be declared the winner. If both boxers are injured, or are knocked out simultaneously and cannot continue the contest, the judges shall record the points gained by each boxer upto its termination, and the boxer who was leading on points, up to the actual end of the contest, shall be declared the winner.

(ii) Winning by retirement

If any boxer retires voluntarily owing to injury or other cause, or if he fails to resume boxing immediately after the rest between rounds, his opponent shall be declared the winner.

(iii) Winning by RSC

RSC is a term used to stop a bout when a boxer is outclassed or is unfit to continue. RSC (referee stopping the contest) term may be used in the following manner:

A) Outclassed   : If, in the opinion of the referee, a boxer is being outclassed or is receiving exessive punishment, the bout shall be stopped and his opponent shall be declared the winner.

B) Injury : If, in the opinion of the referee, a boxer is unfit to continue because of injury, the bout shall be stopped and his opponent shall be declared the winner. The right to decide the result rests with the referee, who may consult the doctor. It is recommended that the referee checks the other boxer also for injury before he makes his decision.

(iv) Winning by disqualification

If a boxer is disqualified, his opponent shall be declared the winner. If both boxers are disqualified, the decision shall be announced accordingly. The disqualified boxer will not be entitled to any prize, medal, trophy, grading or any type of award relating to any stage of the competition in which he has been found disqualified.

(v) Winning by knock-out

If a boxer is 'down' and fails to resume boxing within 10 seconds, his opponent shall be declared the winner by a knock-out.

(vi) No-contest

A bout may be terminated by the referee inside the scheduled distance owing to a material happening outside the responsibility of the boxers or the control of the referee, such as the ring becoming damaged, the failure of the light supply, exceptional weather conditions etc. In such circumstances the bout shall be declared "no contest" and in the case of championship, the jury shall decide the necessary further action.

(vii) Winning by walkover

Where a boxer represents himself in the ring fully attired for boxing and his opponent fails to appear after his name has been called out by the public address system, the bell sounded and a maximum period of three minutes has elapsed, the referee shall declare the first boxer to be the winner by a 'walkover'.

Skills

Sharp reflexes, speed and the ability to concentrate and commit to two minutes of intense, one-on-one combat. Boxer trains to be able to score maximum points with well placed hits to target areas, while also dodging and blocking the blows of an opponent.

Karate

History

Karate translates from Japanese as '*Empty Hand*'. It is a form of unarmed self-defence which first evolved during the 16th century on the island of Okinawa. Denied the right to carry weapons by overlords, the Okinawans secretly developed a system of combat which relied on the power of their hands and feet. The sparring form of karate involving two opponents in combat, delivering kicks, punches or blocking one another's blows, is called *Kumite*.

Another form, using a set of movements and techniques as if in combat with an imaginary opponent, is called *Kata*. A *Karate* tournament may comprise *Kumite* or *Kata* competitions.

Competition area

Competition area must be 8 x 8 metres. It is a flat and matted area which may be elevated to a height of up to one metre above the floor. A referee's line shall be marked 0.5 metre long. It is drawn 2 metre from the centre of the area and two lines are drawn at right angles to this, each one metre long and 1.5 metre from the centre. These are the positions for the competitors. A line of one metre is drawn on the inside of the competition area and the area enclosed by it may be in a different colour.

Dress

White, unmarked GI is to be worn by each competitor, comprising jacket and trousers. This must cover at least two-third of the shin. One contestant wears a red belt, the other wears a white belt. Mitts and gumshields are compulsory and boxes and soft shin pads may also be worn. Shin/Instep protectors are forbidden. To avoid any kind of injury, fingernails must be kept short and contestants must not wear glasses or any other potentially dangerous objects. Degrees of achievement are recognized by a colour of the contestant's belt – the highest being the black belt which, in itself, is divided into ten grades of proficiency.

Starting

Both the contestants take their place on the mat. They used to stand by facing each other with their feet touching their starting lines, bow formally. When they are ready, the referee announces 'Shobu Sanbon Hajime' to start the contest. Each contestant tries to score points by attacking particular areas of his opponent's body. Physical contact is never excessive and certain parts of the body are out of bounds.

Officials

Referee	—	One
Judges	—	Two
Arbitrator	—	One
Timekeepers	—	Two
Caller announcers	—	Two
Record keeper	—	One

Scoring

Scoring is based on the quality of a technique. Each contestant must have a good blowing form. It must be made with good attitude, a good sense of timing and from the correct distance. The result of a bout is determined by either contestant scoring three *ippons*, 6 *waza-ari*, a combination of the two totalling *sanbon*, obtaining a decision, *kiken* imposed against a contestant etc.

A scoring technique counts as a *waza-ari* almost comparable to that needed to score *ippon*. The referring panel must look for *ippons* in the first instance and only award a *waza-ari* in second instance. A victory over an opponent who has been given a *hansoku* or *shikkaku* will be worth *sanbon*. If one of the contestants is absent, withdraws, the opponent will be declared as winner. No technique will be scored if technically it is correct, if it is delivered when the two contestants are outside the competition area. However, if one of the contestants delivers an effective technique while still inside the competition area and before the referee calls '*yame*', the technique will get the point.

Ippon

Ippon is a scoring technique which is performed according to the various procedures like good form, correct attitude, vigorous, *zanshin* (perfect finish), proper timing, correct distance etc. It must be noted that an *Ippon* is worth two *waza-ari*. An *Ippon* may also be awarded for the techniques deficient in one of the basic criteria but which conform to the following schedule:

(i)   Scoring to the unguarded back of the opponent and deflecting an attack.

(ii) Delivering a combination technique, the individual components of which each score in their own right.

(iii) Jodan kicks or other technically difficult techniques.

(iv) Sweeping or throwing followed by a scoring technique.

(v)   Successfully scoring at the precise moment the opponent attacks.

Prohibition

For the sake of safety, the contestants may only attack certain target areas on the body. These include the head, neck, face, abdomen, chest, back and side. They must not attack in such behaviours which are prohibited in the contest. The following are forbidden:

(i)   Direct attacks to arms, legs, face, groin, joints or instep, hips etc.

(ii) Techniques which, by their nature, cannot be controlled for the safety of the opponent, techniques which make contact with the throat.

(iii) Any discourteous behaviour from a member of an official delegation can earn the disqualification of the offender or the entire team delegation from the contest.

(iv) Techniques which make excessive contact having regard to the scoring area attacked. Any technique which impacts the head, face or neck and results in visible injury must be penalized.

(v)   Repeated exits from the competition area or movements which waste too much time.

(vi) Wrestling, pushing or seizing without an immediate technique.

Penalties

(i) *Atenai Yoni* : Imposed for intending minor infractions or may be treated as the first warning.

(ii) *Keikoku* : For infractions not sufficiently serious to merit *hansoku-chui*. In this penalty, a *waza-ari* is added to the opponent's score.

(iii) *Hansoku-chui* : Imposed for infractions for which a *keikoku* has previously been given in that bout. One *ippon* is added to the opponent's score.

(iv) *Hansoku* : Imposed following a serious infraction. Opponent's score being raised to *sanbon*.

(v) *Shikkaku* : Disqualification from the competition. It may be invoked when a contestant commits an act which harms the prestige and honour of *karate* and when in other actions are considered to violate the rules of tournament.

Self-defence

There are some basic tricks which could be further developed and modified into many other tricks. One can modify these tricks to suit his changed circumstances. To protect yourself from the assult of road-side hoodlums, a few effective tricks are given below:

(i) When your opponent is pushing you backwards with his full power, you should check his assult by your hands. Then keeping your one hand on his chest and the other on his waist pull him mutually in opposite direction by giving him a push. He would fall on his face.

(ii) When your opponent is pushing you backwards with all his power, hold both his hands firmly and resist him forcefully. Then seizing your opportunity move backwards all of a sudden and pull him towards you. He would bend himself to regain his lost balance. At the moment, jamming your one leg against his body, pull him quickly with a severe jolt. He would crash headlong on the floor.

(iii) If a hoodlum (*gunda*) tries to put his hand in your pocket secretly then don't panic or lose your heart. Grasp his wrist firmly and give him a severe blow by your other hand in his elbow. He would be constrained to loosen his grip. Then twist his hand from behind. Thus he would be totally in your control. Now give him a severe kick in the knee joint from behind. He would fall on the floor on his back with his leg bent.

(iv) It is an effective trick against eve-teasers. If any hoodlum holds a girl in a lonely spot on the street by her waist from the front, free your hands from his arm-folds and hit his nose with both your fisted hands. Under these circumstances the best defence is your thoughtful assult, however mild. Since he would not be mentally prepared for it, your blow will unnerve him, more psychologically, and he would free.

(v) If an antisocial element tries to snatch the chain from somebody's neck, then he/she should immediately try to free his/her hands and push both his arms sideways. This will loosen his grip on your throat and at that moment he/she should give a severe blow on his nose. He would run away for dear life.

(vi) When your opponent clutches your body in the back-fold, you should bent your one leg and kick him hard in the knee joint. As soon as his grip loosens, thrust him sideways with both of your hands and free yourself. Then hit his stomach with your belt elbow with immense power to overpower him.

(vii) When your opponent comes behind you and catch you in a scissor-fold, you should give him a severe blow on his knee-joint by holding your bent leg. This will loosen his grip. Then raise your hands high and hold his forehead in your grip and broaden your shoulders. In the process, thrust your pointed elbow at your opponent's ribs. He would writhe in pain and you would be free.

(viii) If your opponent clutches your hair from the front, press his hand there itself. Then clutch his hand in the fold of your arm-pits and keep your hand raised high, applying more pressure on his pressed hand. He would not be able to bend his head and would be forced to bend his body down. Then give him a severe jab on his neck to unnerve him completely.

Skills

Overall fitness is crucial, but warming up and stretching exercises prior to any karate practice are essential in order to avoid any injury. Years of hard work and self-discipline are required to acquire a black-belt. Speed techniques and strength are the key components of karate expertise. The beginners must first acquire the basic chops, punches, kicks and blocking. The next step is to learn a series of combinations of these basic techniques.

The key to success in competition is a finely-tuned control over the delivery of kicks and punches as well as a keen sense of timing, alertness and the ability to surprise.

Billiards

History

The game of billiards is known as a 'table game'. Billiards is a game of skill played with three balls and a cue on an 8-legged table having six pockets on it. It is believed that the origin of this game was around 17th century. It is known that Louis XIV was having the billiard table in those days and he used to play the game. His friends, soldiers and servants used to take interest in the game and spread its popularity to other people. The game became popular in France as well as in England and then in India.

In India, the British used to play the game and it became popular amongst the Indian people. India's Wilson Jones was the first world champion. He beat Leslie Driffield in the final of 12th World Amateur Championship in Kolkata in 1958. Jones again won in 1964 at Pukekohe.

Nowadays billiards is played all around the world. It is very popular amongst the young generation in schools, colleges etc.

Equipments

Billiard Table : The billiard table is made with a fine and expensive wood. The table is rectangular in size with a length of 12 ft and a width of 6 ft. Other specifications are as follows:

No. of legs of the table	=	8
No. of netted pockets	=	6
Height of the table from floor	=	2 ft. 9½ inches

2 ft. 10½ inches

State of bed of the table	=	12 ft. x 6 ft. 1½ inches
Playing surface	=	11 ft. 8 inch x 5 ft. 9½ inch

with overhang 11 ft. 9 inch x 10 ft. 5 inch.

A line is marked across the table width parallel with the bottom cushion, exactly 29 inches from its face. This is called the 'Baulk Line'. From the centre point of this line, a semi-circle shall be marked with a radius of 11½ inches. This is known as 'D' and when the player is 'in hand', he must take his stroke from the 'D'. The centre of the table itself is called the 'Centre Point'. Halfway between the centre spot and the face of the top end cushion is called the 'Pyramid spot'. From the face of the cushion twelve and three quarter inches is called 'Billiard spot'.

The Ball : There are three balls used in billiards: One is plain white and one spotted white and third is red. The balls are made of a hard plastic or fibre with a diameter of $2_{1/16}$ inches. All the three balls must be equal in size and weight. Today most of the balls are made of a chemical compound, which displayed *ivoru* during the late' twenties.

The Cue : Cue is a long stick made with wood. This is of two types – long and small. The long cue is used to hit the ball on long distance and small cue is used to hit the ball on short distance. The long cue must not be less than 3 ft. long and consisting of a tapering piece of wood, generally 'Asher Maple'. The 'Butt-End' of the cue should be over one inch. The cue gradually tapers to a round top, on which a leather tip is glued. This end is used to stroke a ball. A piece of white chalk is necessary for roughening the tip surface after every two or three strokes.

Game

To decide which player takes 'Spot' or 'Plain', both either toss up or string for the privilege, although, apart from personal fancy, there is no real advantage in playing with one ball or the other. Winner of the toss plays or he may request his opponent to do so. There are following types of games which are played:

(i) 'Losing Hazard' : This kind of game is played by most amateurs. The player aims at making as many losing hazards as he can, with cannons and pots to leave such strokes when a loser is not practicable. It is a combination of hazards and cannons. This game is also known by the name of 'All-Round' play.

(ii) 'Close-Cannon' : In this game whereby the player scores a sequence of cannons with the three balls close to the cushion. Not more than 75 'direct' cannons must be made.

As stated before very few players are masters of this game. Only by close cannon play can such a sequence be made. In the open sequences of more than 3 or 4 cannons are rarely made. This game is also known by the name of 'Nursery Cannons'.

(iii) 'Top-of-the-table' : A combination of pots of the red ball and cannon-play with the billiard spot as the focal point of the strategy. A favourite 'top of the play' position is – the player cannons sends the red ball towards the opposite pocket for a pot and then tries to leave another cannon of similar type from the other side of the table. This alternate pot-and-cannon play, however, is extremely difficult and generally an extra pot from the spot or a second cannon comes into the scheme. This game is more difficult than other games.

Duration

There are mainly two systems to regard the duration of the game:

(i) The winner is the player who leads after the expiration of a certain period of time i.e. 1 hour, 2 hours, 4 hours – composed of two 2-hour sessions.

(ii) The winner is the player who reaches a fixed number of points i.e. 100, 250 or 500 etc.

Scoring

The main object of billiards is to score more and more points than the opposing player. Points are scored by means of three strokes. They are:

(i) *The Cannon* : A cannon is scored by the player striking his ball with his cue tip and causing to contact the other two balls i.e. the opponent's white and the red or vice versa, in turn, 2 point.

(ii) *Losing Hazard* : A losing hazard is made by striking the cue ball and causing it to enter a pocket after contact with one of the other two balls. A 'loser' off the ball object-white scores 2 points; off the red ball, 3.

(iii) *The Pot* : This is also called the '*Winning Hazard*'. This is made by striking cue-ball to contact one of the two object-balls and cause the object-ball to enter a pocket. For 'potting' the white, the player scores 2 points and for potting the red, the player scores 3 points.

Referee

Like so many other games, a referee is appointed to superintend the game. He is the sole judge of conformity to or infringement of the rules. In big games he is assisted by a marker who controls the score board. The referee not only spots the players but takes the balls out of the pockets for them. He also hands the rest to the player when needed and always calls the score. The referee must declare all fouls directly, as he perceives them. If he has not seen any stroke, he may ask nearby spectators for confirmation of the particular occurrence. He must award a free ball immediately for the players on appeal.

Rests

There are certain positions in which favourable access to the cue-ball is difficult or impossible. For these, a 'rest' is provided. It is a metal cross at its end enabling the cue end to slide normally i.e. on the bridge made with the player's hand. There are short and long rests for each of which a long cue is provided. There are also positions in which the player cannot contact his cue-ball easily because of the closeness of another ball in front of it. To surmount this difficulty, the player uses '*Spider Rest*', which is a cue-slide of extra height.

Baulk Area

A player, whenever 'in hand', must play out of the 'D' from some point within it, that is, he must play away from baulk and not into it. If one or both the object-balls are in the baulk area, the cannon be played at directly. If one ball is in and the other is out of the baulk area, the player may play at the latter but not at the former. It follows, therefore, that if no chance of a score exists, the player can obtain an advantage, and the initiative, by potting the white ball, and placing the red and cue-ball in baulk so that his opponent should fail to disturb them by his stroke out of baulk, he may have a losing hazard left.

Strokes combining side with top or return

While plain striking suffices for a large number of strokes, side and attributes are essential for very others and they are often employed in combinations. Perhaps the most common example of such two elements being employed together are drag and side, and screw and side; but such matters belong to the advanced side of the games.

Restrictions

(i) A player must not make more than 15 winning or losing hazards in succession; after this he must make a cannon or lose his turn.

(ii) If a player runs a 'coup' it is a foul and forfeits 3 points and the non-striker can then have the balls spotted if he wishes.

(iii) Having the white ball spotted after 15 hazards can only occur if the non-striker does not have the balls spotted after the foul i.e., running the '*coup*'.

(iv) A ball line is one that rests on the baulk-line and cannot, thereafter, be played at directly by a player 'in hand'.

(v) A player must not make more than 75 consecutive direct cannons; after this, the break shall only be continued by the intervention of a hazard or a cannon in conjunction with a hazard.

(vi) A player may seek the referee's decision on a point of fact. He may not ask him for what amount to advise.

Fouls

(i) If a ball is forced off the table.

(ii) If the stroke is made before the balls have come to 'rest'.

(iii) If a player plays his ball into baulk when '*in hand*'.

(iv) If any player plays with the wrong ball.

(v) A miss is a foul unless the striker is 'in hand' and there is no ball out of baulk.

(vi) If the cue-ball is pushed with the cue, instead of being struck.

(vii) If a stroke is played with both feet off the floor.

(viii) If a ball is touched other than with the cue-tip.

(ix) If any player plays with the cue-ball touching an object ball.

When the foul is awarded by the referee, the opponent

has the option of playing from the position of the balls left as a result of the foul, or of having the balls spotted and playing from hand.

Skill

The skill of the billiards consists of attaining a high standard of stroke play i.e. ability to perform the various types of strokes. The players must also have the ability to controlling the ball with strokes with the requisite degree of strength and accuracy to ensure a favourable position for another scoring stroke. A favourable position for scoring is called a 'good leave' and an unfavourable position is 'bad eave'. Artistry, therefore, is accuracy plus nicely-gauged ball control. The game is an excellent practice to improve your positional play sense.

Swimming

History

Only vague records of early swimming exist but they indicate that swimming grew up with man from the early stages of his appearance on the earth. When early man needed to move on land he either walked or ran; when early man needed to move across the water, he probably waded, and then eventually swam by watching the example set by other primarily land-based animals. The ability to swim, however poorly, would probably have been part of the dexterity of early hunters, and the need to hunt would certainly have been a reason to swim. In 2500 B.C. the Egyptians produced the first hieroglyphics of the featured swimming. The photograph shows that a swimmer lying flat with one arm out in front and another behind, indicating that even almost 3500 years ago people propelled themselves in water with alternating movements.

Probably the first reference to possible swimming race came in 1595 when Sir John Packington, one of Queen Elizabeth-Ist's courtiers, had a wager with three other courtiers that he could swim from Westminster to London Bridge quickest. In 1615 Queen Anne paid her second visit to Bath and declared that it did her good. She prompted her son Charles I, and his queen to continue this trend a few years later. This was the origin of the spa swimming. In 1603, it was made compulsory in schools and colleges of Japan and various swimming competitions were organised.

English swimming came on 11 August 1873 when John Trudgeon brought both arms over the water in a 160-yard handicap race at Lambeth Baths. He kept his chest high over water and his body flat on the top. He swung his arms alternately over water and with each alternate arm pull he made one horizontal breaststroke kick. Lot of swimming clubs were introduced at that time. The Serpentine Club claiming to be the oldest swimming club (1860).

In 1869 the Metropolitan Swimming Association (MSA) was formed. It changed its name later to the London Swimming Association. Capt. Mathew Webb of England became the first person to cross the English Channel in 1875. Swimming was introduced in Olympic Games in 1896, when the first Olympics were held at Athens. Women's swimming was introduced in Olympics in 1912. In 1908 the Federation Internationale de Natation Amateure (F.I.N.A.) was formed in London during the Olympic Games at the instigation of George Hearn, who asked participating nations to attend a meeting to examine problems with the nature of amateurism. The Ligue Europeene de Natation was founded in 1927.

Swimming Pool

Swimming is a very low-cost sport and the important thing required in this sport is only a pool. You can swim for as long as you want in a public pool for as little as 30 p. Specifications for international pool are as follows:

Length : 50 metre when touch panel automatic officiating equipment are used with starting end or additional on the turning end, the pool must be of such length that ensures the required distance of 50 metres between the two panels.

Width : 21.0 metres (minimum)

Depth : The depth of the swimming pool should be a minimum of 1.8 metres over all for Olympic Games and other world championships.

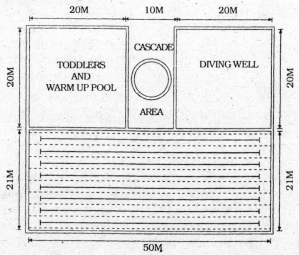

Lanes : There should be a total number of 8 lanes in a pool. The width of each lane should be 2.5 metres with two spaces each of 0.5 metre width outside the lanes number 1 and 8. The lanes shall be separated by ropes extended across the full length of the pool and attached at each end wall through anchor brackets. Each lane rope consists of float placed end to end having a minimum diameter of 5 cm to a maximum of 11 cm. The colour of the floats extending for a distance of 5.0 m from each end of the pool shall be distinct from the rest of the floats. In the centre of each lane a 46 m long and 0.20 – 0.30m wide lane should be marked in contrasting colour. This land should end at a distance of 2 m from the end walls with 1 m long cross line.

Gutters: Gutters may be placed on all four walls of the pool. End wall gutters if installed must allow for attachment of touch panels to the required 0.3 m above the surface of the water. All gutters should be equipped with adjustable shut-off valves, so that the water may be kept at a constant level and they must be covered with a suitable grill.

Water temperature : The temperature of the water in the swimming pool should be +24°C or 77° F. The water must be kept at a constant level, with no appreciable movement. In order to observe health regulations in force in most countries, inflow and out flow of water is permissible as long as no appreciable current or turbulence is created.

Platforms : Swimming competitions are started from the platforms. These platforms must be firm and give no springing effect. The height of the platform above the water surface may be from 0.5 m to 0.75 m. The surface area must be at least 0.5 x 0.5 m. It should be covered with non-slip material.

Equipments

Swimming requires very little equipments. The main expense in competitive swimming is coaching. Many swimmers pay monthly coaching fees which in other sports may have been spent on equipment.

Swimming costume : The most fundamental piece of equipment is the swimming costume itself. The heavy woolen or all-nylon costumes that we once knew are very much a thing of the past. A man's costume needs to be lightweight with a cord for tightening the waist. The greater the costume area, the greater the potential for resistance. The costume should be cut away at the crutch to allow unrestricted leg movements. Woman's swimming costumes need to be free enough at the shoulders allowing them to be able to rotate and move in any direction. It should be comfortable and should not rub on the inside of the armpits and side of the chest, particularly for those swimmers training over distances.

Goggles : Goggles are a very important part of the equipments of swimming. Many swimmers find that long time swimming causes eye irritation and it is therefore important to be able to swim with goggles. The goggles are made of plastic. The eyepiece is with strong elasticated support which goes round the back of the head. Lightweight goggles are very much successful and there are anti-fog varieties which do not mist up. All swimmers should kept a spare pair of goggles. Never put the plastic strap around the back of the head first and the eyepiece on after. Always put the eyepiece over the eyes first and then whilst holding it over the eyes, stretch the elastic over the back of the head.

Floats : A float is an important artificial aid at all levels of proficiency. Cork floats have now faded out because the polystyrene or foam polystyrene are now commonly used. These floats are easy to handle both for legs-only and arms-only drill or attempting lengths or repetitions on both.

Flippers : The flippers are made of plastic with rubber strips. These strips are attached to them. As with all aids, the use of flippers should be counterbalanced with at least as much practice again without them. Flippers help in both loosening up and overloading the ankles on alternating technique.

Armbands : Arm supports are the province of the learner. The double-chamber armbands are secure because if one chamber loses air suddenly for any reason, the other chamber can help the swimmer to stay float.

Pull buoys : A pull buoy can be placed on either side of the legs and can get the body into the correct position in the water more easily. The pull buoy is made of two cylindrical pieces of polystyrene, attached with two ropes for lifting the feet high and close to the surface. Generally, pull buoys are kept above the knees but can also be kept between the ankles. American swimmers use a tubing system known as the *Donnut.*

Earplug : Earplugs used to be literally plugs. These help to prevent water entering the ears and are most useful for swimmers who find it difficult to balance the pressure of air and water in the ear region. The ears should be dry and warm before inserting the earplugs and the swimmer should make sure that the inside of the ear is thoroughly dried after removal.

Nose clips : Nose clips are useful for swimmers who are unable to balance the pressure of air inside the nose with the pressure of water outside. The nose clip is consisting of a plastic clip which presses in a U-shape over the nostrils and an elastic band which wraps behind the back of the head.

Freestyle swimming

Freestyle swimming is also known as Frontcrawl. The modern freestyler is encouraged to keep his body centre on a long axis in line with the direction in which he is moving. A competitor may swim with any style, except that in individual medley or medley relay events. In freestyle swimming, turning and finishing the swimmer can touch the wall with any part of his body. A hand touch is not obligatory. In this style, the swimmer generally breathes on one side. The whole body movement should be almost screw-like in orientation, moving through a lower plane of 180°. The concept of the perfectly flat body position produces a smooth body surface moving through smooth particles of water, in much the same way as a screw failing to grip.

Backstroke

For swimmers who are just learning, backstroke has the advantage of their being able to keep the face away from the water and they therefore find it easier to breathe. In

Rules of Various Sports

competitions, the swimmer should line up in the water facing the starting end, with the hands placed on the starting grips. The feet, including the toes, should be under the surface of the water. Standing on the gutter and bending toes over the lip of the gutter is prohibited. On receiving the starting signal the competitor push away from the wall. Any competitor leaving his normal position of the back before the head, foremost hand, or arm has touched the end of the course, for the purpose of turning or finishing, shall be disqualified. The head position therefore needs to be comfortable, relaxed and the weight of the head should be borne by the water so that the head is never carried above the surface. The swimmer has finished the race where any part of the body touches the wall at the end of the course.

Breaststroke

Breaststroke was the first competitive stroke and it therefore follows that there have been more changes to this stroke than any other. It started like—as a relaxed form of swimming with the head up, and as a stroke which could be used for swimming distances. The body shall be kept perfectly on the breast and both the shoulders shall be in line with the water surface from the beginning of the first arm stroke after the start and on the turn. All movements of the leg and arms shall be simultaneous and in the same horizontal plane without alternating movement. Both hands shall be pushed forward together from the breast, and shall be brought back on or under the surface of the water except at the start and at the turn, the hands shall not be brought back beyond the lip line. The swimmer should breathe once in every arm stroke.

Butterfly

Butterfly can be called as the sister stroke of the freestyle, although the relationship stops there. Butterfly is the most graceful stroke of all the other strokes and this grace can often be accompanied by great power. Both arms must be brought forward together over the water and brought backward simultaneously. No alternating movement of the arms is permitted. The shoulders must be parallel at the surface of the water. Up and down movements are permitted. Alternating movements of the legs are not permitted. When

touching at the turn or on finishing a race, the touch shall be made with both hands simultaneously, and with the shoulders in the horizontal position. The touch may be made above or below the water level. The muscles employed for these movements are very similar to those movements used in freestyle. The power of the pull underwater is developed by internal rotation of the humerus.

Medley swimming

Medley swimming requires the all-round ability of the decathlete in track and field, although the similarity stops there. It is often said that the individual medley favours breaststrokes because it is the slowest and therefore easier to make up more headway. In medley relay events each competitor swims one stroke for the set distance; the order is backstroke, breaststroke, butterfly and freestyle. It finishes when a competitor touches the wall or pad with any part of his body. Each relay team member shall leave the water immediately upon finishing his leg except the member.

Competitions:

Swimming	Men		Women	
Freestyle	50 m, 100 m,		50 m,	100 m,
	200 m, 400 m,		200 m,	400 m,
	1500 m		400 m,	800 m,

Backstroke	100 m, 200 m,	100 m,	200 m
Breaststroke	100 m, 200 m,	100 m,	200 m
Butterfly	100 m, 200 m,	100 m,	200 m
Individual Medley	200 m, 400 m	200 m,	400 m

Relays

Freestyle	4 x 100 m,	4 x 100 m,
	4 x 200 m	4 x 200 m
Medley	4 x 100 m	4 x 100 m

Officials

The organising committee appointed by the promoting authority shall have jurisdiction over all matters not assigned by the rules of the referee, judges or other officials and shall have the power to postpone events. The governing body is required to appoint, subject to the approval of the FINA bureau or the respective regional or international authorities, the following officials for the control of all championships of Olympic Games, world championships, regional games and important international fixtures:

Referee	—	1
Starter	—	1
Chief Timekeeper	—	1
Chief Judge	—	1
Finishing Judges	—	3 per lane
Inspector of Turns	—	1 per lane at both ends
Judges of Strokes	—	2
Announcer	—	1
Recorder	—	1
Clerk of Course	—	1

For all other competitions:

Referee	—	1
Starter	—	1
Timekeeper	—	1 per lane
Finishing Judges	—	1 per lane
Inspector of Turns & Strokes	—	1 for every 2 lanes
Recorder	—	1

Medical control

The FINA International Sport Medicine Committee has

formulated some regulations with the instructions of the I.O.C. Commission, adopted in 1972. The medical control programme at competitions will be under the supervision of a commission consisting of 5 physicians. All selected competitors may be undergoing a medical control test and shall be handed over a notification from/ by a member of the medical commission after the end of the competition. The test of any competitor, if found positive, he will be immediately disqualified from further competition. No smoking is allowed in the territory of the indoor pools including the stands for spectators.

Athletics

History

Athletics is the oldest form of organised sport and enjoying global popularity. Athletics developed with human development. Athletics is not a game but a collection of many competitive events. It is as old as man and got its birth when man started to walk. Running, jumping, prancing and leaping are very common to all human beings and when the element of competition surfaced in their minds, that heralded the advent of athletics. Since ancient Greece gave prime importance to a man's physical attributes and powers. this discipline developed well there. That is why Greece is believed to be the progenitor of athletics.

Track and field athletics date from the ancient Olympic Games. The earliest accurately known Olympiad dates from July 776 B.C., at which celebrations won the foot race. The oldest surviving measurements are a long jump on 7.05 metre by Chionis of Sparta in C. 656 B.C. and a discus-throw of 100 cubits (about 46.30 metre) by Profesilaus. The Lugnased (Tailtean Games) are thought to have been founded as far back as 1829 B.C., some four and a half centuries before the Olympic Games, they are believed to have been started in Greece. Throwing and jumping have been found in human beings from time immemorial. They are part of his struggle for survival. As a sport, jumping and throwing were introduced in ancient Greece in Pan-Hellenic Games in 1864. These games were included in modern world competitions between Oxford and Cambridge in UK.

Today athletics is the central core of the Olympics. In several other games like Asiad, South American Championship, Commonwealth Games, Pan African Games, Caribbean Games etc, athletics is a common event. Women were not allowed to participate in athletics until 1928 Olympics. The world body controlling athletics, the International Amateur Athletic Federation (IAAF), was set up in 1913.

Track and lanes

The length of a track shall be 400 metres (440 yards). It should be at least 7.32 metre (24 ft. wide, representing six running lanes widths, where each lane is 1.22 metre (4 ft.) wide. Lanes may be a maximum of 1.25 metre in width. There shall be eight lanes in a track in big events and there should be an adequate marking of the inner edge of the track. For cinder and other permanent tracks, this should be by a raised kerb at least 5 cm wide and up to 5 cm. in height. Alternatively the inner border can be marked with a 5 cm wide white line, flagged or coned at intervals of 5 m to prevent competitors treading on the line itself. All lanes shall be marked with white colour. Lanes should be measured 20 cm outwards from their respective inner borders in the case of the inner edge of the track, if there is a raised kerb.

The direction of running should be left-hand inwards. The competitors may stay in their own lanes in the races up to 400 metres. In other races a competitor can change his lane. A single finish line should serve all races at the end of one straight.

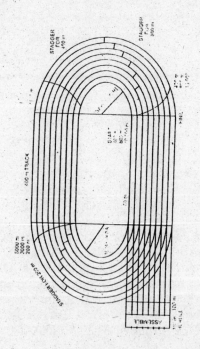

Rules of Various Sports

Track events

Races:

(i)	Short Distance Running	100, 200 and 400 metres
(ii)	Middle Distance Running	800 and 1500 metres
(iii)	Long Distance Running	5,000 and 10,000 metres for men 3,000 metres for women
(iv)	Marathon	42,195 metres (26 miles 385 yards)
(v)	Hurdling	110 metres and 400 metres for men 100 metres and 400 metres for women 3,000 metres steeplechase for men
(vi)	Relays	4 x 100 metres and 4 x 400 metres
(vii)	Walking	20,000 and 50,000 metres for men

(i) Short Distance Running

In such races, a competitor is most dependent on his reaction to the gun, the acceleration away from the blocks and maintenance of his top speed right through the tape, because for him hundredths and perhaps even thousandths of a seconds are vital. He must be able to concentrate his whole consciousness into exploding from the blocks at the gun. The competitor should keep close to the inside line of his lane, and in races not run in lanes there is a very strong case, tactics permitting, for running close to the kerb. Although a runner has been too wide of the inner limit of his lane, this is allowed for because the measurement of total distance run is made 0.3 metre from the kerb or 0.2 metre from the outer edges of the lines marking the other lanes.

In the running of 200 metres, a competitor needs also control, balance and poise. The blocks are placed in the outside of the lane, pointing at a tangent to the curve, so that the first few strides are run in a straight line. The actual start is the same as in 100 metres though the athlete may have other competitors behind or ahead of him in the echelon, which ensures that each other runner has the same distance to cover.

It is very important for the 400 m runner to judge pace and to be able to assess his own ability in relation to the competitors. This race is for the well-trained athlete. It is better to run each 200 m in 25 seconds and 27 seconds than in 23 seconds and in 30 seconds. It is the total time that counts even if that last example ended with 29 seconds. The first 200 m is generally run faster than the second because of fatigue.

(ii) Middle Distance Running

The division between short distance running and middle distance running and between middle distance running and long distance running have become blurred because of the emergence in recent years of the super athlete who, although, specializing can hold his own against more mortals in the 200 m and is a danger to all who consider themselves 10,000 m specialists. Three types of endurance required by the competitor are:

A) Aerobic endurance to utilize as great a proportion of inspired oxygen as possible.

B) Strength endurance to maintain the quality of the muscles contractile forces.

C) Speed endurance for coordinating the speed of contraction in the climate of endurance factors.

(iii) Long Distance Running

Middle and long distance athletes aften suffer from a peculiar addiction – running! The coach may find he has to dissuade his runners from going out for yet another run when all the indications point to rest. After the start, an athlete must run quite fast in first 200 m to achieve good position and it may be necessary to shorten the strides for this purpose. Bend running principles have to be balanced against the tactical advantage of running wide just behind the right shoulder of the athlete in front. The leading runner has the advantage of being able to run on the very inside of the inner lane and yet he may even have to sacrifice this by moving slightly wide on the bends to discourage attempt at passing.

(iv) Marathon:

The marathon race shall be run on made-up road. When traffic or similar circumstances make it unsuitable, the course, duly marked, may be on a bicycle path or foot-path alongside the road, but not on soft ground such as grass, verges or similar thing. A certificate from qualified doctor may be accompanied within 30 days of the race to take part in marathon. There shall be refreshments at the end of first 11 kms and there after every 5 kms. A competitor can not carry any type of refreshment along with him. The distance in kilometres and miles shall be displayed on the route. The members of the organising committee must take care to ensure safety of the competitors.

(v) Hurdling

The hurdle races are run in lanes. The hurdle in each lane is set out in accordance with the specifications. It shall be placed on the track so that 30 cms of the top bar, measured from the inside edge of the track, will be inside the field. The hurdle is made of metal and wood and consists of two bases and two uprights supporting a rectangular frame reinforced by one or more crossbars. The uprights are fixed at the

extreme end of each base and the hurdle should be so placed on the track that the ends carrying the uprights are on the side of the competitor's approach. Each competitor must go over or through the hurdles.

Dimensions of hurdle:

Length	—	70 cm
Width	—	122 cm
Width of top bar	—	7 cm
Thickness	—	1 cm – 2.5 cm
Overall weight	—	3.6 kg – 4 kg

Steeplechase

There shall be 28 hurdle jumps and 7 water jumps included in the 3000 m event and 32 hurdle jumps and 8 water jumps in the 2 miles event. The water jump shall be fourth jump in each lap. If necessary, the finish line shall be moved to another part of the track. The distance from the starting point to the commencement of the first lap shall not include any jumps, the hurdles being removed until the competitors have entered the first lap. It is not possible therefore to lay down any rule specifying the exact length of a steeplechase lap or to state exactly the position of the water jump. Disqualification should result if a runner steps to one side or the other of the water jump, or if he or she trails a foot or leg below the horizontal plane of the top of any hurdle at the instant of clearance.

Dimensions of hurdle:

Height	—	91.4 cm for men
		76.2 cm for women
Width	—	3.96 m
Weight	—	80 kg – 100 kg

Hurdle at the water jump should be 12.7 cm square.

(vi) Relays

Relay races are for teams of four runners. Each runner is carrying a baton for a given distance or stage before passing it to the next team runner. He hands over the baton to the other runner. The baton must be carried out in the runner's hand throughout the race. If it is dropped, it must be recovered by the runner who dropped it. Once a team started in a competition, only two additional athletes may be used as team substitutes for subsequent rounds. A substitution may only be made from among those athletes already entered for the meeting. It is permissible for the order of running to be changed between heats and succeeding rounds or final. No competitor may run two sections for a team.

The lines for the relay races shall be drawn across the track to mark the distances of the stages and to denote scratch line. Lines shall be drawn to before and after the scratch line to denote the takeover zone within which lines the baton must be passed. These lines are to be included in the zonal measurements. In races up to 4 x 220 yards members of a team other than the first runner may commence running not more than 10 metres outside the takeover zone. A distinctive mark shall be made in each lane to denote this extended limit. The last runner, in particular, must know his opposition well if he is to take the initiative early in his leg and decide to take the lead.

(vii) Walking

Walking events include track walks of various limitations. During the whole competition the contestants are required to maintain unbroken contact with the ground. The rear foot should not leave the ground before the advancing foot is placed on the ground. The walker must momentarily straighten his leg when a foot is on the ground.

Field events:

Field events at an outdoor meeting comprise jumping and throwing disciplines – high jump, pole vault, long jump, triple jump, shot put, hammer throw, discus throw and javelin throw. The field events, where the aim is to out-jump or throw farther than the other contestants, a draw should first be made to decide the order in which the contestants compete. Brief details of the above mentioned events are as follows:

(i) High Jump:

The uprights should not be moved during the competition unless the referee thinks that the take-off and landing areas have become unsuitable. The competitor must take off from one foot. Knocking the bar off the supports or touching the ground or the landing area beyond the plane of the uprights with any part of his body without clearing the bar shall count as a failure. Competitors are not required to wear shoes with a sole thickness of more than 13 mm or a heel thickness over 19 mm. A competitor may take the maximum of 15 m runway and the landing area should measure not less than 5 m length and 3 m in width.

Specifications:

a) *Uprights* : The uprights should be sufficiently tall so as to exceed the maximum height to which the crossbar can be raised by at least 10 cms. The distance between the uprights shall not be less than 3.66 m and not more than 4.02 m.

b) *Crossbar* : The crossbar shall be between 3.64 m and 4 m. The maximum weight of the crossbar should not be more than 2 kgs.

c) *Supporters* : The supporters for the crossbar shall be rectangular consisting 40 mm width and 60 mm length. Both supporters shall face the opposite upright. Space between the end of the uprights and crossbar shall be at least 10 mm.

(ii) Pole Vault:

A competitor aims to clear a high crossbar with the aid of a long and flexible pole. He holds the pole a little way from its top, along a runway towards the uprights and digs the end of the pole into a box sunk below ground level. The competitor swings upwards towards the bar, arching over it feet first and face down before dropping on to a thick, soft pad. The pole vault box shall be made of wood, metal or similar thing. The width of the box must be 60 cm at the front tapering to 15 cm at the bottom of the stop-board. Any competitor is not allowed to touch the pole unless it is falling away from the bar or uprights. If it is so touched and the referee is of the opinion that it would have caused the bar to be displaced, the vault shall be recorded as failure.

Any competitor may use his own pole. But it must be fit according to the specifications of the organising committee. A competitor becomes fail if he knocks the bar off the supports, he leaves the ground for the purpose of making a vault and fails to clear the bar, after leaving the ground places his lower hand above the upper one or moves the upper hand higher on the pole and before taking-off touches with any part of his body with pole, ground including landing area, beyond the vertical plane of the upper part of the stop-board.

Specifications

A) **Uprights :** Except where extension arms are used the distance between the uprights shall not be less than 3.66 m and not more than 4.32 m wide.

B) **Cross-bar :** The length of the cross-bar shall be between 3.86m to 4.52 m and it shall consist of a weight of at least 2.26 kgs.

C) **Supporters :** Pegs shall be used to support the cross-bar and shall be without notches or indentations of any kind. The thickness should not be more than 13 mm. Supporters must not extend more than 75 mm from the uprights and the crossbar shall rest on them so that if any competitor touches it or his pole, it will fall easily to the ground in the direction of landing area.

D) **Pole :** The pole may be of any material or combination of materials and of any length or diameter, provided that the basic surface is smooth. It may have a binding of not more than two layers of adhesive tape of uniform thickness and with a smooth surface. The restriction does not however apply to binding the bottom end of the pole with protective layers of tape for a distance of about 30 cm to reduce the risk of damaging the pole when striking the back of the box.

(iii) Long Jump:

A competitor must prepare himself in a related condition for the take-off. The action at the take off board involves the roll of the foot from the heel to the ball. The body should be plunged up with the chest and chin up, the back slightly

arched and the feet trailing behind. The feet should keep about a foot apart and bring the body forward between the knees to ensure throwing the body forward beyond the point where the heels strike the pit. The competitors are judged to have failed a trial if they touch the ground beyond the take-off line with any part of their body; in the course of landing, touch the ground outside the landing area at a point nearer to the take-off than the nearest break in the sand by the jump take-off from outside either end of the take-off board, whether beyond or before the extension of the take-off line.

Specifications

Take-off board : It should be made of wood or some rigid material. The length of the take-off board should be 1.22 m and the width should be 200 mm. It should be 100 mm deep. A horizontal shelf should be fixed on the side nearer to landing area. It should be 1.22 m long, 100 mm wide, the top should be 38 mm below the surface of the take-off board. The take-off board shall be painted white.

(iv) Triple Jump:

A competitor tries to clear the longest distance following a sprint along a runway up to a take-off board. The triple jump involves a more complicated hop, step and jump sequence of actions before similarly landing in the sand. In addition to the training done as a competitor the triple jumper must devote much of his training time to "ploymetrics" – the explosive type eccentric muscles contraction work of depth jumping. The examples of this training method are as follows:

A) Jumping from the top of the box.

B) Jumping from the top of the box to the floor, immediately rebounding from one or both feet to another box to the floor, to a box etc.

C) Hopping or double foot bounding, over low hurdles placed about 2 m apart.

D) Vertical jumps in rapid sequence while holding dumb-bells.

In triple jump the hop is made first so that the competitor lands first upon the same foot as that from which he has taken off. If he touches the ground with 'sleeping leg' while jumping, it shall be considered as failure. The other rules are as applicable as for the long jump.

(v) Shot Put:

The shot is a heavy and cannonball-like ball. It is held in one hand against the side of the chin and propelled by pushing it away from the body—actually throwing it is against the rules. As for all throwing events, different weights are used for men, women and for different age groups. A competitor must commence the throw from a stationary position within the circle. No competitor may place, or cause to be placed, any mark within the throwing sector. The competition does not allow any competitor to wear any gloves and no device of any kind i.e. taping of fingers.

In making his puts the competitor may rest his feet against but not on top of the stop-board. Each competitor

may have two practice trials before the competition begins. The shot shall be put from the shoulder with one hand only. At the time the competitor takes a stance in the ring, the shot shall touch or be in close proximity to the chin and the hand shall not be dropped below this position during the action of putting. All the measurements shall be made immediately after each put. A competitor should not leave the circle until the shot has touched the ground. When leaving the circle, the first contact with the top of the circle rim or the ground outside the circle has to be completely behind the white line which is drawn outside the circle and runs theoretically through its centre.

Specifications

The shot should be made of any metal not softer than brass, or a shell of such metal filled with lead or other material, with a smooth finish. It must be spherical in shape and no unorthodox shot surface is permissible. The minimum weight should be 7.26 kg for men and 4 kg for women. The diameter for men's competitions is 110 mm and for women competitors 95 mm. The interior of shot circle should be constructed of concrete, asphalt or similar firm and nonslippery material. The circle rim should be made of band iron, steel or other suitable material. The diameter of the circle should be 2.135 m.

(vi) Hammer Throw:

The implement used is not a conventional hammer but a metal ball attached to a wire which has a handle at its other end. The competitor grips the handle with both hands and begins by whirling the ball around in a circle. Passing above and behind the head and just below the knees. The thrower then spins around three or four times within the throwing circle, building up centrifugal force, before releasing the hammer upwards and outwards. The grip, stance, swing and the pivot and the turn are the basic techniques of hammer throw.

The throw shall be made from a throwing circle of 2.135 m in diameter. Using of any types of gloves is not permitted. The competitor in his starting position prior to the preliminary swings or turns is allowed to put the head of the hammer on the ground outside the circle. If the head of the hammer touches the ground when the competitor makes the preliminary swings or turns, but if, after having so touched

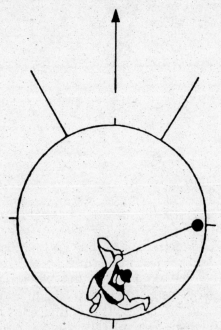

Rules of Various Sports

the ground, he stops so as to begin the throw again, they shall count as trial throws; it shall not be considered a foul throw. If the hammer breaks during a throw while in the air, it shall not count as a throw provided it was made in accordance with rules. If the competitor thereby loses his equilibrium and commits a foul, it shall not count against him. A competitor must not leave the circle until the hammer has touched the ground. A throw is measured from the nearest indentation in the ground made by the head of the hammer to the inside of the circumference of the throwing circle, along a line drawn to the centre of the circle.

Specifications

(A) **Head** : The head shall be of solid iron or other metal. If filling is used this must be inserted in such a manner that it is immovable and that the centre of gravity shall be not more than 6 mm from the centre of the sphere.

(B) **Handle** : The handle of the hammer shall be of single spring steel wire. It should be unbroken and straight not less than 3 mm or No.11 standard wire guage in diameter. It shall be such that it cannot stretch appreciably while the hammer is being thrown. The handle may be looped at one or both ends as a means of attachment.

(C) **Grip** : The grip may be either single or double loop construction. It must be rigid and without hinge joints of any kind, and so made that it cannot stretch appreciably while being thrown. It must be attached to the handle in such a manner that it cannot be turned within the loop of the handle to increase the overall length of the hammer.

(D) **Cage** : The hammer throw cage shall be made of an enclosure. The cage should be capable of stopping a hammer moving at a speed of up to 32 m per second and should be so arranged as to eliminate any danger of ricocheting back towards the athlete or over the top of the cage. The diameter of the cage should be of 7 m with the opening through which the throw is made 6 m wide. The height should be 3.35 m to 4 m. The whole cage must be covered with net of 19.2 m long and 0.3 m wider than the height of the struts, made of cord 12.5 mm in circumference with 50 mm meshes. It is suspended from the wire cable or series of metal struts. The 8 metal supports are set into the ground with permanent sockets which sink to the depth of 30 cm. The supports and suspended net are kept in position by wire ropes attached to ground spikes.

(vii) Discus Throw:

Discus throw requires a well-developed body, large and strong hands, long arms and perfect agility. It requires proper neuromuscular coordination of a very high order to be a good discus thrower. The athlete holds the discus against the palm of the hand and forearm of the throwing arm, with the finger-ends around the edge. Facing away from the direction of the throw the athlete then rapidly makes one and half spins before propelling the discus into the air with a side-arm throw.

The competitors are not permitted to wear gloves in their hands nor apply any substance on their shoes or in the throwing circle. A competitor should not leave the circle until the discus has touched the ground.

It is a foul if, having started to make the throw, a competition touches the ground outside the circle or the top of the circle rim with any part of his body. For a throw to be valid the discus should land completely within the inner edges of lines marking a sector of 40°. If the discus breaks during a fair throw, it should not count as a trial.

Specifications:

(A) Discus : The discus shall be made of wood or other suitable material with a metal rim. The edge of the rim should be identical, without any indentations or projections. The minimum weight of the discus should be 2 kg for men and 1 kg for women. The outer diameter of the metal rim should be 219 mm to 221 mm for men and 180 mm to 182 mm for women. Diameter of metal plates should be 50 mm to 57 mm for men and women. It should be 44 mm to 46 mm thick for men and 36 mm to 37 mm thick for women. The thickness of the rim at a distance of 6 mm from the edge should be 12 mm for both men and women.

(B) Circle : Most of the other specifications for the discus circle are the same as those for the hammer circle except that the inside diameter of the circle should be 2.5 m.

(viii) Javelin Throw:

In the ancient times, hunting with throwing of spear was a very popular and common game. The event, javelin throw, is a developed technique of the same. The javelin should be held in one hand only, and at the grip, so that the smallest finger is nearest to the point. Two parallel lines mark the javelin runway and competitors, during their run-up to throw, may not cross either of these lines. A competitor may not turn completely around so that his or her back is towards the throwing arc of the scratch line, until the javelin has been launched. If a competitor steps on or beyond the arc, or extended scratch line in the course of a throw, it should be recorded as a foul.

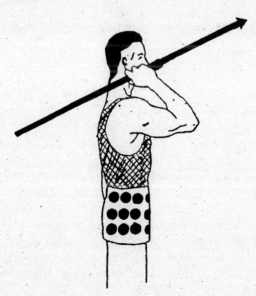

No throw shall be valid in which the tip of the metal head does not strike the ground before any other part of the javelin, or when the competitor touches, with any part of his body or limbs, the strip or the lines drawn from the extremities thereof at right angles to the parallel lines or the ground beyond those lines or the strip. The competitor may cross either of the parallel lines.

The javelin shall be thrown over the shoulders or upper parts of the throwing arm and must not be slung or hurled. It must also be within the inner edges of the landing sector. When the javelin has touched the ground, the competitor may leave the runway from behind the white line of the arc at right angles to the parallel lines. If the javelin breaks in the air during a fair throw, it shall not count as a trial provided the throw was made in accordance with the rules. The measurement should be recorded in even centimetres units to the nearest point below the distance measured if that distance is not a whole even centimetre.

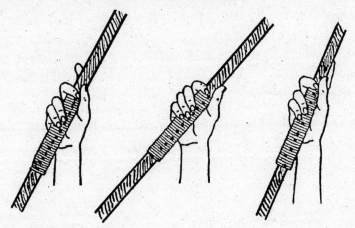

Specifications

(A) Javelin : A javelin comprises a shaft of metal with a pointed metal head fixed to it and a cord grip. The finish of the shaft should be smooth and uniform. The cord grip, covering the javelin's centre of gravity, should not exceed the diameter of the shaft by more than 8 mm. The cross section of the javelin should be regularly circular throughout, the maximum diameter of the shaft being immediately in front of the grip. From the grip, the javelin should taper regularly to the tip at the front and the tail at the rear. The weight of the javelin should be 800 gms for men and 600 gms for women inclusive of cord grip. The overall length for men should be 260 cm to 270 cm and for women 220 cm to 230 cm. The length of metal head should be 25 cm to 33 cm for both men and women. The distance from tip of metal head to centre of gravity should be 90 cm to 110 cm for men and 80 cm to 95 cm for women. The diameter of shaft at thickest point should be 25 mm to 30 mm for men and 20 to 25 mm for women and the width of cord grip for men should be 15 cm to 16 cm and for women 14 cm to 15 cm.

General Books

LITERATURE

Iqbal Ramoowalia
The Death of a Passport 150.00
Mainak Dhar
Flash Point 195.00
Gurdial Singh
Earthy Tones 95.00
K. R. Wadhwaney
Scandel Controversies &
World Cup 2003 ....195.00
Dr. Giriraj Sah
Human Rights 195.00
A. K. Sharma
Clinton Levisky Scandal 60.00
Nostradamus and Prophecies
of the next Milleneum........................195.00
Jaisankar Prasad
Kamayani 50.00
Brindawan Lal Verma
Toote Kante.......................................150.00
Aditi
My Endless Journey 50.00
Rabindranath Tagore
Boat Accident
(Translation of नौकाडूबी) 95.00
Inside Outside
(Translation of घरे बाइरे) 95.00

HISTORY AND BIOGRAPHIES

Lokesh Thani & Rajshekhar Mishra
Sensational Sachin 60.00
K.R. Wadhwaney
Scandals and Controversies
of World Cup 2003 ....195.00
Virendar Kumar
Kargil : The Untold Story Rape of
the Mountain (With Pictures) 95.00
R.N. Sanyal
Freedom Struggle of India 95.00
Dr. B. R. Kishore
Chess for pleasure 60.00

Joginder Singh
Without Fear or Favour 195.00
Discovery of Independent India 195.00
B. K. Chaturvedi
Power to power 30.00
Chanakya Neeti 95.00
Kautilya's Arthashastra 95.00
Famous Tourist Centres of India 95.00

BIOGRAPHIES

Meena Agrawal
Indira Gandhi 95.00
Rajiv Gandhi 95.00
B. R. Kishore
Neelkanth (Lord Shiva)........................95.00
Gajanan 95.00
Hanuman 95.00
Goddess Durga 95.00
Lord Buddha 15.00
Lord Rama..15.00
Lord Krishna.......................................10.00
Asha Prasad
Swami Vivekanand 120.00
Mahesh Sharma
Ramkrishna Paramhans 95.00
Dr. A.P.J. Abdul Kalam 95.00
Atal Bihari Vajpayee 95.00
Lal Krishna Advani..............................95.00
Dr. Bhawan Singh Rana
Chhatrapati Shivaji.............................95.00
Bhagat Singh 95.00

FICTION

Abhimanyu Unnuth
Slices from a Life *(Memories of*
great writer of Mauritius)....................**95.00**
R. N. Vyas
A New Vision of History......................195.00
Swaran Chandan
The Volcano
(A Novel on Indian Partition)..............195.00

◎ Fusion Books

X-30, Okhla Industrial Area, Phase-II, New Delhi-110020, Ph.: 41611861, Fax: 41611861,
E-mail: sales@diamondpublication.com, Website: www.diamondpublication.com

Some books which you will love to read

BOOK OF LOVE

By: Maria Shaw

Rs. 150/-

Find out with this fun guide to love and friendship. What should I wear on a first date? Is Libra a good match with Aries? How can I find out if someone wants to go out with me. Discover how to get answers to all of your relationship questions with Maria Shaw's Book of Love. Easy to use and fun to read, this unique guide to relationships gives you:

* An astro compatibility guide for each sun sign.
* Quick and easy magical how-to's.
* Palm reading tips and techniques.
* Simple formulas for determining love number compatibiltty.

SPIRITUAL FITNESS

By: Nancy Mramor

The simple exercises and techniques presented in Spiritual Fitness are not tied to any specific spiritual tradition and can be practiced by anyone. They are designed to lead you toward greater contentment in all areas of your life:

* Improve your physical, emotional, and mental health
* Free yourself from negative behaviours that block happiness
* Discover how to find lasting inner peace
* Deepen your spiritual awareness

Rs. 95/-

HOW TO HEAL WITH COLOR

By: Ted Andrews

Rs. 95/-

How to Heal with Color shows you how to use the vibrational effects of color to heal yourself and others. Learn how to:

* Use colors to balance the chakras
* Determine therapeutic colors by muscle testing
* Apply color therapy through touch, projection, breathing, cloth, water, and candles
* Rid yourself of toxins, negativity, and patterns that hinder your life process
* Use the powerful color-healing system of the mystical Qabala to balance and open the psychic centers
* Perform long-distance healing on others

For vibrant physical, emotional, mental, and spiritual health—add color to your life.

THE INSTINCT TO HEAL

By: David Servan-Schreiber

Heal is a powerful word. Isn't it presumptuous for a physician to use such a word in the title of a book on stress, anxiety, and depression? I've thought a lot about this question. To me, "healing" means that patients are no longer suffering from the symptoms that they complained of when they first consulted, and that these symptoms do not come back after the treatment has been completed. This is what happens when we treat an infection with antibiotics. The ideas presented in this book are largely inspired by the works of physicians and researchers.

Rs. 195/-

◎ **Fusion Books**

X-30, Okhla Industrial Area, Phase-II, New Delhi-110020, Ph.: 41611861, Fax: 41611861,
E-mail: sales@diamondpublication.com, Website: www.diamondpublication.com